MOBBED UP 2

Lock Down Publications and Ca$h
Presents

Mobbed Up 2

A Novel by *King Rio*

Lock Down Publications
P.O. Box 944
Stockbridge, Ga 30281
www.lockdownpublications.com

Copyright 2021 by King Rio
Mobbed Up 2

First Edition August 2021
Printed in the United States of America

This is a work of fiction. Names, characters, places, and incidents either are products of the author's imagination or are used fictitiously. Any similarity to actual events or locales or persons, living or dead, is entirely coincidental.

Lock Down Publications
Like our page on Facebook: Lock Down Publications @
www.facebook.com/lockdownpublications.ldp
Book interior design by: **Shawn Walker**
Edited by: **Jill Duska**

Stay Connected with Us!

Text **LOCKDOWN** to 22828 to stay up-to-date with new releases, sneak peaks, contests and more…
Thank you!

Submission Guideline.

Submit the first three chapters of your completed manuscript to ldpsubmissions@gmail.com, subject line: Your book's title. The manuscript must be in a .doc file and sent as an attachment. Document should be in Times New Roman, double spaced and in size 12 font. Also, provide your synopsis and full contact information. If sending multiple submissions, they must each be in a separate email.

Have a story but no way to send it electronically? You can still submit to LDP/Ca$h Presents. Send in the first three chapters, written or typed, of your completed manuscript to:

LDP: Submissions Dept
P.O. Box 944
Stockbridge, Ga 30281

DO NOT send original manuscript. Must be a duplicate.

Provide your synopsis and a cover letter containing your full contact information.

Thanks for considering LDP and Ca$h Presents.

Prologue
Saturday, December 26th, 2015
Chicago, Illinois
8:39 AM

Rell got the best wakeup he'd ever in his life experienced, from the beautiful black woman he'd only known for two days now, but was quickly growing to love.

At first he thought he was dreaming.

The suction on his dick felt too pornstar-ish to be real.

Slowly, he forced his eyelids to separate, and squinting against the sunlight that was pouring in through the parted curtains, he looked down and realized that it wasn't a dream after all.

Tamera Lyon's lips were wrapped tight around his huge erection, and her head was bobbing rapidly. There was saliva sliding down the sides of his stone-hard phallus. Her hands were busily working, stroking his length and massaging his scrotum.

He chuckled once, wiping the gunk from the corners of his eyes.

"If these are the kind of wakeups I'ma be gettin', we can go and get married today," he joked, scooting back and sitting up.

Tamera moved with him, keeping her mouth locked on his love stick. She was in her bra and panties. The bedroom door was wide open, because there was no need to worry about intruders. They were in the house that Rell's father, David "Big Man" Owens, had bought for him and Jahlil, his younger brother. It was a duplex home, and Jah had his own place upstairs.

The room was bare except for the five-piece bedroom set Big Man had already had here when Rell and Jah arrived and the sheets, blanket, and pillows Rell had taken from his bedroom at his mother's house.

He cast a quick glance at the nightstand to make sure his Glock pistol was still there and saw that it was laying just as he'd left it before going to bed last night, with its long 30-shot clip jutting out toward him and its barrel pointed to the door. Beside it lay his smartphone and a pile of cash that amounted to just a few hundred dollars under $4,000. The money had come from Big Man, and it was all the money Rell had to his name.

His attention went back to Tamera.

Her head was almost a blur.

"Damn. Keep goin' just like that," he said, his lips spreading into a grin. He fingered a couple of strands of hair from over Tamera's face so that he could get a clear view of her oral skills. "That's that shit I like, baby. You can wake me up like this every fuckin' morning. You hear me? Every morning. Suck this dick like it disrespected you or somethin'. Make it throw up. Do you, baby."

He leaned back on the pillows and watched the show, and a moment later his eyes moved to the sparkling diamond ring Tamera was wearing. It was a $100,000 engagement ring, with a round-cut 9 carat white diamond. It was on her ring finger, but she wasn't engaged. The ring belonged to Susan Owens, Rell's stepmother. Susan had accidentally left the ring at hers and Big Man's apartment before leaving for a two-week vacation in Florida. She was currently waiting on Rell to express mail the ring to her.

The ring looked good on Tamera's finger.

She must have noticed that he was looking at the ring. She slid her left hand up his herculean chest and gazed at it herself as she continued to fellate him.

"You might get one of these from me one day," Rell said, thrusting into her mouth as he felt the familiar tingle in his scrotum of an imminent eruption. "Keep treatin' me like this and...you gon'...have me in the palm of your...hand."

He barely got the last word out. Tamera took her mouth off him and stuck out her tongue. His semen spurted out in four long ropes, three of which landed in stripes on Tamera's face. There was more, but she sucked the head in her mouth and gently bobbed her lips on it until the flow ceased.

"Yes, my nigga," Rell said with a laugh as he watched her get up and saunter out of the bedroom. "You are the greatest."

Chapter 1

Robin's Jean clothing seemed to be the style of the day. Tamera had already taken an early morning bath. She put on a skintight pair of grayish-blue Robin's jeans and an equally snug sweater that Rell had bought for her yesterday. Big gold hoop earrings dangled from her ears as she stood over the stove cooking breakfast.

After taking a shower, Rell put on a new black hoodie, shirt, and jeans by the designer, along with a black pair of Timberland boots and a black Louis Vuitton belt that he'd owned for a while, but still looked relatively new. A spray of Cool Water cologne and the feel of the Glock on his hip completed his look, and seconds later, he stood in front of the mirror feeling like a new man.

The scent of sizzling meat made his stomach grumble as he was checking his smartphone. He had a voicemail message from Maria, his mother, and two more from Erica, a girl he'd been occasionally sleeping with for the past two years.

"Get out here and eat, boy," Tamera shouted from the kitchen.

Rell was contemplating a way to tell Erica it was over as he walked out of the bathroom. There was no way he was going to give up on the blossoming romance with Tamera. He'd always wanted a woman like her, and he'd be damned if he was going to lose her over a woman as promiscuous as Erica.

He sat down at the large oak dining room table, which had eight matching ladderback chairs situated around it. Big Man had handled most of the furnishings, but there were a bunch of things Rell would need for his new home.

"You don't have a broom or a mop," Tamera said as she brought his plate to him. "And you need to go to the store for some more pots and pans. Your daddy must have just bought one set for you."

"We'll get all that shit later," Rell said. What mattered now was his growling belly.

Tamera had good skills when it came to cooking. The beef sausages were on point, and so were the pancakes, scrambled eggs, and grits. She put a glass of cold milk next to his plate and then sat across from him with her own plate and glass of milk.

Rell thought, *So, this is what it's like to have a good woman.*

Erica had never woken him up in such a great way, and she most certainly wasn't going for cooking and preparing a plate for him.

"Let me know if you want seconds. There's some more left," Tamera said.

Rell nodded his head and kept eating. The food was deliciously flavorful, and he ended up getting a second helping. While Tamera was refilling his plate, he dialed his mother's mobile phone number, a part of him already knowing what the call would be about.

"You know the cops just left up outta here," Maria said. "Askin' about you and Jah. They want y'all to go down to the station and talk to 'em about that boy who got killed in my alley."

"I'm not going to no police station, Ma. You already know that."

"Well, hell, what happened out there, Rell? Huh? Tell me. 'Cause I was dead sleep, and the next thing I knew it sounded like a damned war out back. Somebody needs to tell me somethin'. Tell me if I need to be worried about some niggas comin' back to my house tryna kill y'all. You can at least tell me that much."

"Ma, I don't know what to tell you. Some niggas got to shootin', a nigga got whacked. That's all I know."

"They say it was two men, Rell. Two. One got found in a shot-up car somewhere down on Independence. Did you do that to them? Tell me now, Rell. Don't let me find out when ya ass is in the county jail."

"I ain't shot nobody, Ma."

"You lyin', Rell. You lyin', and the truth ain't in you. And what's with this new girl Jah's sleepin' around on Felicia with? Who is she? Felicia came over here cryin' her eyes out talkin' about some girl she caught Jah messing around with."

"Ma, stop askin' me all these questions. Are you okay? Do you need somethin'? I'm eatin' breakfast right—"

"Yep, I need a sack and a bottle."

Rell burst out laughing. Momma consumed more weed and liquor than he did. He couldn't count on both hands the number of times she'd smoked him under the table.

"A'ight, I got'chu, Momma. Gimme an hour or so and I'll be over there."

"Keep that pistol on you," Momma said. "And make sure your brother keeps his on him, too. It's getting crazy out here, and I'd rather be visiting you two in jail than burying your asses. If anybody kill my babies, it's gon' be me."

"What?" Rell was incredulous. "What the...what kinda...Ma, you crazy. Bye. Be over there in a minute."

Rell ended the call, shaking his head and grinning at his mother's fucked-up logic.

He ate his second plate and then went to the bathroom to brush his teeth again. Tamera came in behind him with her head down, digging through her Michael Kors purse.

"We need to go to Walmart, Rell. To get the stuff for the house first and foremost, but I need some things for myself."

"That's why you got a car."

"Don't do me, Rell." Tamera raised her eyes to the mirror and rolled them at his reflection.

Her beautiful chocolate brown face made him smile. She stood next to him and brushed her teeth. He kept glancing at her ass. It looked amazing in the tight jeans. She had a true phatty, perfectly round and so meaty that the back of her jeans could not completely cover it, which left the top of her panties exposed.

He thought of the way she and her sister had beat up Tirzah's boyfriend yesterday and his smile broadened. Tamera was most certainly everything he'd ever wanted in a woman: pretty, loyal, a shade of gangster, and thick where it counted.

"I can't believe my sister got to blasting at Stain like that," she said with a mouthful of Colgate toothpaste. "And he's dead! Do you think one of her bullets did it? Because both of you were shooting."

Rell wasn't sure whether or not it had been him or Tirzah who'd killed Stain, but he wasn't going to take the blame for it, so he just shrugged and gargled a capful of mouthwash.

There were other things to worry about, like the beef he and Jah — along with the other guys from their block — now had with the gang on 16th and Millard. So far, his gang was winning. Over the past couple days they'd killed and wounded several of their enemies, but Rell knew that it was only a matter of time before his gang would take a loss. He was determined to make sure he and his little brother were still standing when it was all said and done.

He and Tamera left out of the bathroom together and put on their leather Pelle Pelle jackets. His was black and hers was gray. She had on a pair of gray Jordan sneakers that went along perfectly with her jacket.

He'd anticipated going upstairs to wake up Jah, but was surprised to find Jah and Tirzah sitting in chairs on the front porch, smoking blunts with Apple, a fat guy who lived across the street.

There was at least a foot of snow piled up on the ground, and it was cold enough to necessitate a pair of gloves.

"Are you niggas slow?" Rell said in disbelief.

"Man," Jah said, dropping his head back to look at Rell, "it ain't that cold. Here, hit the dope." He passed Rell a blunt. "Apple say them niggas on Millard got money on our heads. I gave Lil Larry this address. He on the way over with them choppas. Johnny B just bonded out. It's crackin', bruh. Let a nigga pull it if they wanna. We knockin' tops off."

"On Neal." Rell hit the blunt, giving Trumbull Avenue a visual sweep. There was no one on the street, but he was certain that the young mobsters were in one of the alleys, serving whatever drugs were available at the moment.

After a minute or so, Rell got everybody to go and sit in his car, an off-white 2013 Impala. He let the girls take the front seats, with Tamera behind the wheel, and he got in behind her. This way, if anything were to happen, he and Jah could shoot while Tamera sped off.

Apple sat between Rell and Jah, and all three of the guys began rolling blunts of the orangish Hawaiian Kush that Jah had robbed one of Tamera's coworkers for the other day.

Tamera turned on Rick Ross's Black Market album and upped the volume so that it was just loud enough for them to be able to talk and hear each other while listening.

Rell and Jah kept looking in every direction. They both had their guns on their laps.

Apple said, "My sister told me about the money they got on y'all. Some nigga named PJ say he got ten bands on y'all, supposed to be over Stain gettin' whacked."

"Fuck all them niggas," Jah said, picking up his Ruger. It had a 32-round extended clip in it, and he was never reluctant to open fire. "On Neal, they whacked D-Lo. From now on, I'm blowin' every time I see one of them pussy mu'fuckas. I don't care who wit' 'em or who vouchin' for 'em. They slid down on my OG crib, too! Nigga, I'm on that."

Rell nodded. "I'm surprised they still want smoke after all them bodies done got dropped. Niggas see we ain't playin', but this shit can keep goin' as long as they want it to. I ain't duckin' no nigga."

"No, Rell," Tamera said, turning to look back at him. "We are not looking for trouble. I mean, if it comes, then so be it, but looking for it is a whole different story. Just because they don't have anything to live for doesn't mean we have to be just as careless. I really don't even like us sitting here in broad daylight like this. We need to go somewhere."

"Drive off," Rell said. "We gotta go to Walmart, don't we? Let's go. We'll stop by my momma house when we get back."

"I got some food on the stove," Apple said. He was the kind of chubby guy that everyone loved to be around, always full of jokes and entertaining stories.

"Fuck it," Rell said. "We'll sit here and smoke this loud first." He cast a suspicious glance at a passing Trailblazer, saw that it was K, one of the guys off Trumbull, and gave a head nod.

Apple said, "Shit is gettin' heavy in these streets. First D-Lo, then Martez, then Jamie and Stain. Ray and another lil nigga got shot on Millard. They out here sprayin' shit up, joe. I told my girl yesterday, it's like the west side is turnin' into the south side. It's supposed to be about money, feedin' our families. These young niggas ain't listening, though. All they wanna do is shoot."

"Yeah, it's all bad." Jah laughed. Though he was sincerely upset over D-Lo's murder, the drama excited him. He lived for it. It was quite obvious that he could not wait to pick up his gun and start shooting.

Seconds later, there were three blunts lit. They smoked and listened to Ross preach about what was going on in the streets. There were several shots taken at 50 Cent throughout the album, Rell noticed, but that was to be expected.

Rell could hardly pay attention to the music.

He kept looking from the alley to the street behind him and in front of him, studying every vehicle that drove by. Trumbull was a one-way street, so every passing car faced the same direction as Rell's.

He didn't like that his back was to 16th Street, because it was the busiest street in the neighborhood, and cars kept turning off 16th and onto Trumbull.

Which is why he blew out a sigh of relief (along with a stream of smoke) when Apple finally got out of the car. Jah had to get out first to let Apple out, and he held his gun until he was back in the seat.

Rell hardly noticed that Jah was back in the car; he was looking back over his shoulder, his eyes on a dark blue Delta 88 that was just turning onto Trumbull.

The Oldsmobile came to a sudden stop three houses down from where Rell's car was parked.

Opening his door, Rell nudged Jah with an elbow and snatched up the Glock.

But it turned out to be a false alarm.

A woman and a child got out of the car and headed toward the house it was stopped in front of.

"Damn," Jah said, shaking his head. "Almost aired that mu'fucka out. Let's go."

Tamera pulled off in a hurry.

Chapter 3

"Bruh, somethin' was off about Shalonda when I dropped off that sack to her yesterday. I can't quite put my finger on it, but she seemed different. Like she was scared. I don't know." Jah shrugged his shoulders as he put fire to the end of another blunt full of Kush. "The bitch had me 'noid. Good thing I had this pole on me."

The "pole" Jah was referring to was a Ruger 9 millimeter with a 32-shot extended clip. At the moment, it lay on the lap of his fresh black Robin's jeans as he sat in the backseat of the clean white Impala.

Rell was glad to be sitting next to Jah in the backseat. He had the hood of his black hoodie pulled over his head as the new woman in his life — the beautiful, brown-skinned Tamera Lyon — drove down Douglas Boulevard on Chicago's west side.

Rell's eyes were low and red. It was the day after Christmas, and they were on their way to drop off an ounce of Hawaiian Kush to Marshawn, a guy Rell had gone to high school with a few years ago.

They had just returned from Walmart. The trunk was jam-packed with bags and boxes.

"We gotta take Momma a sack," Rell said, counting out $1,000 cash out of his bankroll. "And I want some of that Kush, nigga. You got two pounds of that shit. Don't trip over Shalonda. She ain't on shit. I mean, shit, don't trust nobody, but I don't think she'll pull it. We know her whole family. And she knows you. She ain't about to risk her life like that."

"She bet' not. 'Cause I'll definitely take that mu'fucka."

Rell dropped the $1,000 on Jah's lap and gazed out his window as they made it to the house where Marshawn lived with his girlfriend on Albany Street.

"What's this for?" Jah asked.

Tirzah looked back at the pile of cash on Jah's lap and said, "For me."

"Pops told me to give you a stack," Rell said. "I want a half pound of that Kush, too. I'll get you back."

"That's the same shit you said last time," Jah reminded him. "And the time before that."

Tamera gave Tirzah a cold stare and said, "Sounds like somebody I know. Always promising to pay a bitch back."

Smiling, Jah added the cash to his own smaller bankroll, and stuffed it in his pocket as he pushed open his door.

He didn't make it out of the car.

Rell grabbed the collar of Jah's jacket. "Hold on, lil bruh. Look. The red Chevy. That's Ray's."

It was an early 90's model Caprice, parked further down Albany, and there were two guys standing next to it.

Ray was one of the guys Jah and his boys had shot a few days ago during the shootout that had cost D-Lo his life.

Jah looked at his big brother with an expression that was as cold as the weather was outside. His fingers curled around his Ruger pistol.

"Stick talk?" he said.

"You already know," Rell replied, and the two of them got out of the car with their guns aimed at Ray and the guy who was standing with him.

The gunshots were thunderous.

Chapter 4

BOOM! BOOM! BOOM! BOOM! BOOM! BOOM! BOOM! BOOM! BOOM! BOOM! BOOM! BOOM!

Ray and his boy didn't stand a chance. The bullets knocked them to the ground before they had a chance to react.

Ray managed to crawl around to the back of his Chevy Caprice, leaving behind a trail of blood. He reached around the rear left tire with a handgun and began shooting back at Rell and Jah.

Instinctively, Rell ran onto the sidewalk and sprinted to the other side of the Caprice as quickly as he could run. He saw that the guy who'd been standing with Ray was lying still in the middle of the street in a burgeoning pool of blood. He also noticed that a little girl who looked to be about eight or nine years old was running away on the sidewalk with a grown woman.

Jah was still shooting, running up the middle of the street, shells falling from his gun as he went.

Rell made it to Ray first.

The guy was already badly wounded. He had on a red jacket that was a shade lighter than his Chevy, and there were multiple bullet holes in it. He was on his stomach, gun in hand, fighting to keep breathing as blood poured out of his wounds.

Without a moment's hesitation, Rell shot him once in the back of the head. Ray's head jerked violently downward, and he didn't move again.

"Bruh, look at this fuck nigga!" Jah shouted. He was standing over the other guy.

It took Rell a couple of seconds to see that the guy was breathing.

"Man, smoke that nigga and let's go!" Rell shouted back as he turned to run back to the Impala.

Just then, he heard a scream.

It was the woman who'd been running with the little girl.

Rell flinched at the sound of Jah's gun going off.

BOOM! BOOM!

He didn't even look to see what Jah had done. His eyes were on the little girl, who was now cradled in the arms of the screaming woman.

The screams would forever be etched in Rell's mind.

Stunned, he ran back to his car and got in just seconds before Jah.

Tamera sped off in reverse and then whipped around onto Douglas Boulevard.

"Damn," Jah said. "I think I...damn."

He didn't need to finish the sentence. Rell knew what he meant.

Jah had just unintentionally shot a child.

Chapter 5

"Ooh baby, now let's get down tonight
Baby, I'm hot just like an oven
I need some lovin'
And baby, I can't hold it much longer
It's getting stronger and stronger
And when I get that feeling
I want sexual healing
Sexual healing, oh baby
Makes me feel so fine
Helps to relieve my mind
Sexual healing baby, is good for me
Sexual healing is something that's good for me

Whenever blue teardrops are falling
And my emotional stability is leaving me
There is something I can do
I can get on the telephone and call you up baby, and
Honey, I know you'll be there to heal me
The love you give to me will free me
If you don't know the thing you're dealing
Oh I can tell you, darling, that it's sexual healing

Get up, get up, get up, get up - let's make love tonight
Wake up, wake up, wake up, wake up - 'cos you do it right

Baby I got sick this morning
A sea was storming inside of me
Baby, I think I'm capsizing
The waves are rising and rising..."

David Owens was really feeling himself this morning. The way he was grooving to the Marvin Gaye song, wearing nothing but a pair of boxers and socks, with one hand on his wrinkled belly and the other in the air as he danced around near the foot of the bed in their hotel suite — it was too much for Susan to bear.

"Turn off that damn music, Dave. It's ten o'clock in the damn morning. I told you not to have that drink."

"It's a vacation, baby. We're supposed to have fun, enjoy ourselves. I didn't get on you last night at the concert, so don't you go getting on me."

Susan had to agree with him there. He'd taken her to see Anita Baker, one of her all-time favorite singers, and she'd just about jumped on stage.

She was sitting up in bed with a Newport cigarette smoldering in one side of her mouth. The eye on that side squinted against the smoke. On her left wrist was a new red diamond tennis bracelet that Big Man had bought for her yesterday, more than likely to keep her mouth shut about the ring.

She wasn't going for it, though.

"You need to be on that phone calling Rell," she said, crossing her bony arms over her chest. "I want my ring."

Big Man stopped dancing and turned to look at Susan. "Do you? Do you really want it?"

"You gon' make me hurt you, Dave."

"No, I'm saying, do you really want it sent here? To a hotel in Miami? Are you out of your mind? What happens if it's stolen? Then what?"

Susan's expression dimmed for a second — this was a prospect she hadn't considered. "Well, get a post office box. Something. We're not about to just leave my ring in Chicago until we get back. That's two whole weeks away. I want people here in Miami to know that I'm married to a good man who purchased me a gorgeous ring four years ago. It's a part of our story, Dave. I feel empty without it."

"I feel empty without the $100,000 I spent on it," Big Man mumbled, just loud enough for Susan to hear as he sat down at the foot of the bed and began putting on his slacks.

If not for the slight pain in Susan's back, she knew that she would have moved toward Big Man and given him a stiff kick for the snide remark.

Instead, she mumbled a response. "Asshole."

He chuckled, and the rolls of fat on his back bounced merrily.

"This weather is amazing," he said. "Been in Chicago my whole life. Never witnessed a hot winter day. We've gotta visit south Florida more often."

"We have to move to south Florida, is what you mean."

"Actually, that's not what I meant."

"Well, it should've been what you meant. There ain't nothing in Chicago but death and destruction. Oh, and snow. Tons and tons of icy fucking snow. And now look at what's happened. Somebody's been killed in our building. Cops are questioning your ex-wife about some guy who was killed in her backyard on the same night. No, Big Man. Hell no. That's not the way I intend to spend the last of my days. If that's what you want, then fine, you can go back by yourself. I'm staying here."

"We've got property in Chicago. What are we gonna do, just leave it there?"

"Hell, you can't take it with you! Dummy. That's why they have real estate agents. Sell the damn things and move on. Bottom line, I'm not going back to Chicago unless it's to get my ring."

"I'll get you your stupid ring, Susan. Sheesh. I'll get it if it's the last thing I do." He got up and headed into the bathroom.

Susan wasn't letting him off the hook that easily. She wanted to make it clear that she meant what she said about not returning to Chicago.

"I'm about to call a moving service," she said. "Call and make sure Rell is around to give them the keys to our place."

"You're being ridiculous, Susan."

"Call it what you want, but I ain't going back to that godforsaken place. You can just find yourself another wife there since you wanna go back so bad. I don't mind."

This time Big Man didn't reply. Susan sat there on the bed, smoking her cigarette and thinking of a way to win this particular argument.

It didn't come to her until ten minutes later, when Big Man came out of the bathroom dressed in a fine blue Armani suit over matching gator-skin shoes.

"I've got an idea," she said, standing up and knowing that she didn't look too shabby herself in the expensive blue dress he'd bought her for the lunch date they would be heading to very shortly.

"Yeah?" Big Man's tie was pulled slightly askew. Susan walked over and fixed it.

"Yeah," she said. "I know that your boys are your pride and joy, and that you just gave them the house on Trumbull Avenue. How about you bring them here to Miami with us for the weekend? Have them fly out today. They can go back Monday morning. We can talk to them about maybe moving here to Miami with us, and we can kill two birds with one stone, because then I'd get my ring back without the worry of it being lost in the mail."

Big Man knitted his brows together. "I don't remember agreeing to moving here myself."

"Oh, yes you do." Susan pecked her lips against his. "If you love me you do."

Chapter 6

When they made it back to the house on Trumbull and into Rell's apartment, Tamera pulled Tirzah into the bathroom for a chat. Tirzah couldn't stop the tears from flowing down her face. She had already been stressing over the shooting at Rell and Jah's mother's house, not knowing for certain if she had killed Stain that night. Now, with the little girl being shot, she was a nervous wreck.

She put her hands on the sink and leaned forward with her head down. "If she died, Tamera. If that girl died..."

"I know, sis." Tamera gave Tirzah's back a consoling rub. "It's okay to cry. I'm crying with you."

And indeed she was. She and Tirzah sobbed their eyes out for a good five minutes before either of them were ready to speak. Tamera hugged her big sister in a snug embrace, and they cried on each other's shoulders.

"She was so young," Tirzah said finally. "No kid deserves to be shot like that. I'm praying she makes it. I'm praying for her to live."

"Me too, Tirz. Me too." Tamera pulled back and thumbed away her sister's tears, while her own tears continued to flow. "It'll be okay. We just...let's just think about it. After this, I don't know if I even want to be around those two. Shit is getting out of hand. I mean, I want love, but not if this is the cost. I'd rather be single than to keep going through this continuous drama. Here, sit down." She led Tirzah to the edge of the bathtub.

"I don't think I can stay with Jah, either," Tirzah said. "He's young and wild. I'm too many years older than him. I've learned stuff that he hasn't, and it's irking my nerves. You can't just go around shooting like that."

"You're right," Tamera agreed.

"Shit's about to hit the fan. With Webb, with those niggas off Millard — I don't wanna be caught in between any of it. Our lives are in jeopardy being here with them right now. There's no telling who knows they live here now. That fat nigga we smoked with has probably told everybody by now."

"We can't blame the situation with Webb on them. That was all us."

"Yeah, but it was still their fault. If we hadn't been fucking around with them, Webb wouldn't have tried to snatch me up like he did."

"That's your fault, sis."

Tirzah sucked her teeth and looked up at Tamera. "Bitch, whose side are you on?"

"I'm just being real, sis. Hell, we might be putting them in just as much danger from Webb and his people as they are with the niggas they got beef with. Nobody's really right here. We're all messing up big time. You're just upset over seeing that kid get shot."

It was true. Tirzah was usually the toughest spirit in the Lyon family, but there were certain things that got to her, and one of them was seeing children hurt.

Tamera sat down on the toilet seat. "Everything will be fine. Let's just think for a minute. Think of what we're going to do next. I think we need to get the fuck away from here for a while. Maybe we should go and visit Ma in Virginia."

"No." Tirzah shook her head. "We're in deep shit right along with Jah and Rell, and I think it's only right to climb out of it with them. We'd be fake as fuck if we did anything else, and you know I ain't no fake bitch. I was just...bothered...by that kid. Jesus Christ. I can't believe it."

"This might not be the best time to tell you this, but I finally got a text from Joseph. He's in the hospital. Jah robbed him for that Kush and beat him with the gun. Broke some bones in his face and knocked out some teeth. I told him it was a guy I'd just met, and that I didn't know his real name."

Tirzah rolled her eyes and shook her head. Jah was only 17, and she was 26. He was just as wild as she'd been at his age. She almost regretted having sex with him. It was practically a case of child molestation. If any of the girls she'd gone to school with learned of their relationship, she knew that she'd be the talk of Facebook. She was used to being the girl that everyone was jealous of. Hardly any of her old schoolmates were as beautiful as her, though many of them were doing better. She had been pretty much broke ever since she quit stripping, and it was times like this that she wished she would have never stopped riding the pole.

"I should go back to stripping," she said abruptly. "Fuck the bullshit."

Tamera scoffed at the sudden shift in conversation. "Where in the world did that just come from? I thought we were grieving over the kid. How did stripping just pop up in your head?"

"I made good money stripping. You remember all that money I used to have. I'm not feeling this doing hair every now and then BS. That's barely enough for weed money."

She took a few squares of tissue off the roll and dabbed her eyes dry. Tamera did the same thing.

"So, what are you saying?" Tamera asked.

"I'm saying that I'm going down to Redbone's to see if they're hiring. It's good money. I need my own car, some new clothes — you know. I'm tired of struggling. With this sexy-ass body I got, why not make some money with it? At least until summer rolls around. If I stay there for a few years, I'll leave with enough money to buy us a house. Whatever I do, I have to do it now. I'm done sitting around smoking weed all day. Life's too short for that. If you wanna go and visit Ma, we can do that, but I'm letting you know now, as soon as we get back, I'm going down to Redbone's to see if I can get my job back."

Tamera stood up and put her hands on her hips. "All I wanna know is how did we go from crying to stripping? Please explain that to me. I am so lost right now."

Tirzah rolled her eyes as she too stood up. She hugged Tamera, sniffled twice, tossed the soggy tissue in the small trashcan next to the toilet, and went to the door.

"Come on. Let's go and make sure our lil boy toys are okay," Tirzah said. She opened the door and left out feeling seventy percent better than she had coming in.

Chapter 7

Jah broke the promise he'd made to himself to stop drinking liquor. He poured himself an inch of Hennessy in a glass and swallowed it down in a single gulp as he sat at the dining table.

Pacing back and forth in the living room, Rell was making phone calls to hear what the streets were saying.

Apparently, everyone knew that it had been him and Jah who'd been involved in Martez's, Jamie's, and Stain's murders, but no one had told the cops. Nobody had seen the shooting on Albany Street, but Marshawn (who was still waiting on his ounce of Kush) said that there were three dead bodies — Ray, Ray's cousin Tazz, and an eight-year-old girl who lived down the street from Marshawn named Sapphire.

Jah hardly gave the girls a glance as they came out of the bathroom and joined him at the table. He had a blunt lit but he wasn't passing this one. He needed every bit of THC in it to combat the insurmountable guilt he felt at having shot and killed an eight-year-old.

Tears kept slipping down from his eyes, yet he wore an indecipherable expression. He was drumming the fingernails of one hand on the table and holding the blunt in the other. Thinking back, he recalled seeing the kid fall as he was running up the street shooting. He knew that, judging from where the little girl was running when he saw her, he had to have been the cause of her death.

Tirzah moved her chair closer to his and put her head on his shoulder. He gave no reaction. He only put the blunt to his lips and filled his lungs again, staring vacantly at the short drinking glass that stood between the bottle of Hennessy and his handgun. It had a Chicago Bears helmet printed on its side, just like the rest of the drinking glasses in his and Rell's kitchen cabinets.

"You okay, Jah?" Tirzah murmured worriedly.

Jah gave a half nod. "I'm guwop."

"The hell's that supposed to mean?"

"I'm good," he said.

A tense silence ensued. Rell was now on the phone with Big Man, Jah noticed, but he didn't pay attention to what exactly was being said.

His eyes lifted up a couple of inches to Tamera, who was standing at the other side of the table with her hands on her hips. He stared at the huge diamond ring on her finger. It took him a moment to realize that it was his stepmother's ring. By then Rell had ended the call and walked over to stand behind Tamera, wrapping his arms around her waist.

"Pops wants us to fly to Miami, lil bruh. I told him we had some ladies with us. He said he'll pay for all of our tickets and our expenses when we get there. We can get in our own lil vacation. I think we need it. What you think?"

Jah felt Tirzah's head leave his shoulder but he didn't look at her. He kept replaying the Albany Street shooting over and over in his head.

Tirzah said to Tamera, "I'm with it, sis. Never been to Miami before." She turned to Rell. "We were just talking about how we needed to get away from here for a while. This shit is for the birds. I wanna turn up, have some fun. These past couple of days have been everything but fun."

"I'm all in," Tamera said, nodding her head.

Rell looked at Jah. "Bruh, what's up? You wanna go? We can pack up and go straight to the airport right now if you wanna. I'm tryna see what Miami's like for once. Shit, we need to go somewhere. Anywhere but here. We'll fuck around and be in jail for life by tonight if we don't leave now. We need some time to think over all the shit that's goin' on before we make some mistakes we can't take back, you feel me?"

Jah nodded his head in agreement and poured himself another shot.

He'd never been on an airplane before, and he figured another shot or two of the good old Henny would help him on the journey.

Chapter 8

Tamera and Tirzah had to go to their apartment to pack up their bags.

The four of them climbed back in the Impala, again with Jah and Rell in the backseats, and Tamera drove the two blocks to the yellow brick apartment building on the corner of Homan and Douglas.

During the short ride, Rell phoned Momma and apologized for not bringing her the weed and liquor she'd asked for. She sounded like she was already intoxicated. She rushed him off the phone without even a goodbye.

By the time he looked up from the phone, they were at the building.

He and Jah waited in the car while the girls went up to their apartment. He pocketed his smartphone and stared out his window, because Jah seemed too out of it to keep watch himself.

"We gotta get the fuck away from this shit, bruh," Rell said, watching as Dominique, a pretty girl he'd gone to high school with, waved at him as she drove by in her SUV. "I'm thinking about asking Pops to get us a house down there in Miami instead of the one on Trumbull."

"I ain't moving to Miami," Jah said in a near whisper. "I'll go, but I ain't stayin' for good. I can't fit in down there. I'm a Chicago nigga."

"This shit ain't gon' get us nowhere, lil bruh. For real, for real. Ain't no jobs. Ain't no hope. Just gangbangin' and dope slangin'. I just did years in the joint for living this street life. I want somethin' different. I know it might sound crazy to you, but I wanna get married and have kids and chill with my family all day."

"Who you gon' marry? Tamera?"

Rell hesitated. "Shit, I might," he said finally. "Why you say that?"

"I said it 'cause we just met these hoes, nigga. That bitch Tirzah sucked my dick as soon as she got the chance. I ain't marrying her. I'm seventeen. I'ma fuck that bitch a few more times and bounce."

"That's you, bruh," Rell argued. "I'm grown now, lil bruh. I'm done sleepin' around with every bitch I see. I just want one good woman, and to tell you the truth, yeah, I would marry Tamera. She's the kinda girl I can see myself with in the future. Good personality, beautiful, no kids. Same age as me. I need somethin' good in my life, and the streets ain't gon' give me that. God can only give me—"

"Awww, shit. Here we go with this religious shit."

"This ain't no religious shit, nigga. This some real shit." Rell was getting frustrated with Jah's ignorance. "Name one nigga in the streets that's living the life you wanna be living twenty years from now. Would you rather play a role in *The Wire* or *The Cosby Show?*"

"Bill Cosby was raping mu'fuckas."

"Well, a different show. You know what the fuck I mean. You wanna live a good life or a bad life? The choice is yours, and as a big brother, it's up to me to set a good example for you. I could lead you down the path I was on before I went to the joint, but that's a path straight to hell, lil bruh. I want more than this for us. I want us to be legit millionaires one day. We can get money like Pops and Susan."

Jah shook his head and sighed. He looked around, finally becoming more alert. He dug in his pocket and pulled out a pack of Newport cigarettes and lit one. "Whatever, bruh. You just knocked some noodles loose on Christmas Eve. That street shit is still in you, and it ain't goin' nowhere no time soon. But I'm with you. Whatever you wanna do. I'm not movin' to no mu'fuckin' Florida, but I'm with you on everything else."

Rell sighed and shook his head. There were some lessons that people just had to learn for themselves.

Far down at the end of Douglas, on Albany where he and Jah had ended the lives of Ray and Tazz, Rell could see several CPD squad cars. Some were parked, but one of them was turning to come his way.

"Shit, man, let's get up out this hot-ass car before that cop get here," Rell said, shoving open his door. "Ain't no tellin' if somebody gave 'em the description of it."

Jah tucked away his pistol and stepped out of the car with Rell. They entered the apartment building and stood just inside the glass door. There was a hallway that led to the two first floor apartments to the left and the stairs to the right.

Three teenaged boys were hunched over a crap game further down the hallway. Two of them wore hoodies like Rell and Jah, and the third wore a White Sox skullcap and a sweatshirt. The two in the hoodies had dreadlocks.

"I'm thinkin' about lockin' my shit up," Jah said thoughtfully. "Bitches love niggas with dreads."

"You'll look just like that ugly-ass nigga Chief Keef," Rell joked with a chuckle.

"Fuck you." Jah puffed on his cigarette and gazed out the steel-framed glass door.

Rell kept glancing at the dice game. He never gambled, and he wondered why so many of the young guys in the neighborhood did it. Most of them didn't look like they had any money to spare, so why they took chances with the little they did have never made sense to him.

The hallway reeked of weed and cigarette smoke. There were blunt wrappers and cigarette butts strewn about, and someone had scrawled on the wall with a black marker the letters "TVLN" (which stood for Traveling Vice Lord Nation, one of the Lawndale neighborhood's most dominant street gangs). Beneath the four letters were a long list of RIPs. Lil Charlie, Bay Bay, Red D, Baby James, Scrizzle, and Don P.

Rell had known all of the deceased men. They were victims of black-on-black gun violence, which had long ago become the norm in the Windy City.

Jah noticed that Rell was looking at the wall and started reading it for himself, while Rell thought of Tamera and wondered if she was indeed the kind of woman he'd been wanting for so long, the kind of woman who'd hold him down and be there for him and with him every day and night.

"Can't believe Pops actually owns this whole building," Jah said, jarring Rell from his thoughts. "That's some real boss shit, bruh. Remember, that nigga was a straight up dope fiend. Now look at him. Nigga done gained about two hun'ed pounds. He done stopped using, got married, bought up a bunch of houses — his old ass is winnin'. Wish he would stop being so fuckin' stingy. The nigga treat us like kids."

"We are kids to him. We'll always be kids to him."

"We grown as fuck, bruh. Niggas ain't makin' it to see eighteen around this mu'fucka. Look at this wall. All these niggas died young. Ain't no sense in bullshittin'. If you gon' do somethin' for a nigga, ain't no time like now."

"He just bought us a house, bruh," Rell said. "A whole house. That ain't enough?"

Jah didn't get a chance to answer.

Suddenly, the three teenagers were right up on them.

The light skinned one with dreadlocks had a small-caliber gun aimed at Rell's head.

"Run that bread, nigga!" he said.

Chapter 9

Lil Chris was nervous, but determined to get the huge wad of cash he'd seen Jah's brother with yesterday. He wasn't much younger than Jah, and he knew that Jah was with the shits when it came to gunplay, but none of that mattered to him right now. What mattered was the money.

"You better act like you know who the fuck I am," Jah said, turning to glower at Chris. "All o' you lil niggas know how I'm rockin'. Play this game if you want to."

"Come up off that bread, nigga," Chris repeated, his finger on the trigger. He pushed Zo, one of his friends, toward Jah and Rell and ordered him to go in their pockets.

Both Jah and Rell cast cold stares at Chris as Zo approached them.

"What the fuck is that, a .22?" Jah said. "You tryna stick us up with a mu'fuckin .22? Nigga, are you serious?"

"Shut up, Jah," Rell said.

"Nah. Nah, fuck that. These lil niggas got me fucked up, joe. On Neal. Y'all gon' try to rob us?! Y'all wanna rob the guys?"

Chris didn't expect what came next.

Just as Zo was digging in one of Rell's front pockets, Rell's right hand flew toward Chris's gun. He grabbed ahold of Chris's wrist and pushed his arm skyward just as the gun went off, while at the same time swinging a fist at Chris's jaw.

The punch didn't drop Chris. They struggled over the gun while Jah started fighting with Zo and E.

This wasn't the way Chris had envisioned the robbery going.

He caught two powerful punches to the eye and another to the nose. Dizzied by the blows, he fell back against the wall, still trying to pull his wrist free so that he could take control of the situation.

Rell was as strong as a wrestler. He flung Chris to the other wall and then back to the first one, then punched him in the eye again. Every time Chris tried to swing, he got tossed around and punched.

Panicking, he slipped his index finger in over the trigger and started shooting recklessly, sending bullets everywhere his arm swung, hoping for just one of them to hit Rell.

Then he was suddenly upside down in the air, falling...

Chapter 10

The boy went unconscious as soon as his head hit the floor.

Rell picked up the gun and turned to check on Jah.

The two other boys were running out of the building, and Jah was sitting against the wall, holding both hands over his stomach.

"Bruh, I'm...shot," Jah said.

Rell became furious. He turned back to the unconscious teen and was just about to put a bullet in his head when he heard Tamera.

"Oh, my God, what's going on down here? Were those gunshots? Jah, are you shot?"

She was coming down the stairs with Tirzah, looking leery and worried.

Rell gritted his teeth together. Dropping the pistol in a back pocket, he grabbed Jah's arm and pulled him to his feet. With his other hand, he drew the Glock from his hip. If not for Jah being wounded, he would have chased down the escaping teens and murdered them in broad daylight, and he wouldn't have cared if the cops down the street caught him doing it.

Tamera helped him take Jah to the car, and this time he took to the driver's seat. He heard Tamera say she'd follow him in her car as he sped off down Douglas.

Seconds later, he remembered that there was a triple murder scene up ahead and slowed the car, but once he had made a few turns and was on Roosevelt Road, he stomped on the gas.

"You'll be good, lil bruh. Just breathe," he said, looking over at Jah.

Jah's hands were covered in blood.

"Hoe-ass nigga," Jah said. "Shot me in my goddamn stomach."

Rell couldn't stop gritting his teeth. He was no longer thinking about Tamera or any of the peaceful, law-abiding things he'd been thinking just minutes prior. No; now he was feeling like his old self, the street nigga who'd been one of the TVL's top gunslingers before his stint in prison. He wanted so badly to get his hands on the teens who had just tried him in such a bold way. How dare they try robbing him? He was one of the few real niggas the mob had left. If anything, the youngsters were supposed to look up to him.

A glance in the rearview mirror showed him that Tamera was indeed following, though she seemed to be struggling to keep up.

"Slow down, bruh," Jah said, "before we both end up in the hospital. It ain't that serious. I'm talkin', ain't I?"

"Those bullets travel, bruh," Rell said. "This little-ass gun." He took the gun out of his back pocket and put it on Jah's lap as he slowed down.

Jah chuckled and winced at the same time. "Nigga shot me with this lil piece of shit. I'm killin' dude with this same strap, watch. Fuck nigga. I know all them niggas, too. Zo, Chris, Lil E. All three of 'em gon' get it."

"Aw, don't even trip. They'll be chopped down as soon as I get you to this hospital. I ain't goin' for no nigga shootin' my lil brotha."

Rell's smartphone rang with a call from Tamera. He answered and put it on speakerphone.

"What the hell happened?" she asked.

"Ol' bitch-ass nigga tried to stick us up," Rell said, instantly becoming angrier as he began speaking about the failed robbery. "I slammed the one who upped the strap and knocked him out, but he let off some shots first. One of 'em hit lil bruh in the stomach."

"Jesus, we can't get a break. I guess this means that the trip to Miami's canceled."

"Fuck a trip. I'm sendin' niggas on a trip, a'ight. It won't be to Miami."

"Oh, Lord," Tamera said, no doubt understanding what Rell meant.

He would be sending some niggas to the grave today.

Chapter 11

Susan was seriously debating whether or not she should try and find a hitman to kill her husband.

The way this fat fucker was chowing down on his dish of wood-oven salmon was just rude and disrespectful.

They were seated at a table inside Soyka, an upscale restaurant just east of Little Haiti that had once been a railroad station. The cavernous restaurant was by far Susan's favorite place to eat in Miami, and she had only been here twice.

She had a roasted turkey club that she was almost too embarrassed to eat. With Big Man sitting right across from her, eating his salmon like a starving runaway slave, she was afraid that people would look their way and assume that they were homeless or something.

"It is not that serious, David," she said in disgust as she scowled at him.

He laughed once and dabbed a napkin on his mouth as he leaned back in his chair and looked at her. When he finished chewing he said, "Food is supposed to be eaten, am I right?"

"Yeah, but you're drinking it."

"Drinking it?" Another laugh from the fat guy. "Don't be ridiculous."

"Don't be embarrassing."

"I'm sorry, honey. Want me to eat like a nice little schoolgirl? Is that it?"

"What I want you to do is eat like a regular human being. Eat like someone who doesn't think his plate is about to magically disappear. That's what I want."

"You know, you weren't so bitchy when I first married you. You getting tired of the old man already?"

"You weren't such a pig back then. You're getting worse. And I want my ring."

He grinned and pointed an accusatory finger. "Ah. I see. That's what's bugging you. It's the ring. You're going crazy without it on your finger."

It was true. Susan was so used to seeing the chunky diamond on her finger that she was lost without it. Not to mention it was her most prized possession, the single most expensive thing she owned. The ring was worth more than all of her other jewelry combined.

She rolled her eyes and bit into her turkey, thinking that if Big Man just so happened to die before she did, she would buy herself an even pricier ring to flaunt on her finger as she traveled the world and ate at fine restaurants like this one.

"There's nothing to worry about," Big Man said. "The boys are flying in. I'll be wiring Rell some more cash for the tickets. They should—"

"Wait, did you just say you're sending him more money? After giving him six grand just two days ago? Are you out of your mind, David? You know that the boys Rell hangs out with are all drug dealers. You should never give him that much money. He'll use it to buy drugs. That's probably why the guy got killed in our building. Come on now, Dave. You're smarter than that. Use your head for once."

Big Man moved forward in his seat and squinted at Susan. "As long as I live, my boys will be taken care of. You got that? I neglected them for way too many years as a drug addict, and now I will give them what I should have given them long ago. I could care less what you or anyone else has to say about that. So eat your lunch and let me enjoy mine. Your stupid little ring is on the way."

Susan didn't say another word until they were leaving Soyka ten minutes later, and then it was only to chastise Big Man for not holding the door open for her.

There was a vending machine outside the restaurant that was replete with all the kinds of snacks that Big Man loved to eat. He went to it while Susan headed for their rental car.

As she was getting in behind the wheel, she received a catcall from a passing younger gentleman.

"Hey, hot momma. Where's the ring? I know a fine young woman like yourself can't be without a husband."

Susan looked at the stranger. He was a white man, tall and handsome, possibly in his early thirties, dressed like a lawyer in a nice button-up shirt and tie over slacks and shiny-toed black shoes.

As bad as Susan wanted to engage him in conversation, she knew that Big Man would have a fit, so she settled for a friendly wave and half smile combination.

Wrong decision.

The man turned and walked to her window.

She looked past him and saw that Big Man was staring at the vending machine with his arms crossed over his chest, trying to decide on which snacks he'd purchase.

"You've got great taste in vehicles," the white man said, sweeping his eyes over the Bentley. "I actually have one of these myself. Well, a Bentley. Mine's a Mulsanne. I'm Chuck Calloway, CEO of Hazel Eve Real Estate. Heard of us? We're the second leading real estate agency in south Florida."

Susan shook her head. "No, I'm sorry," she said. "I haven't heard of your company. I'm Susan Owens, by the way. Do you have a business card? My husband and I are actually considering moving here in the coming weeks."

"Your husband?"

"Yes. He's standing over there at that vending machine."

Susan was not certain, but she thought Chuck looked mildly upset by the revelation of her marriage.

A man as handsome as Chuck, upset that an old lady like her was married? Susan was flattered.

He handed her a business card and wished her a blessed afternoon just as Big Man came walking to the car.

Big Man got in with his face all frowned up. He watched Chuck stroll away.

"Who in the hell is he?" Big Man asked.

Susan passed him the business card. "He's the man who's going to help us find a good place to live here in Florida."

And he may be my next husband, she thought, though she knew that she'd never be bold enough to say it to Big Man.

"You gonna call and find out what time the boys will be landing? And did you remind Rell to bring my ring?"

"Yes, Susan. I reminded him to bring the ring with him." Big Man was obviously tired of her questioning him about the godforsaken ring. "Not sure what flight they'll be taking. I'll give Rell a call now."

Chapter 12

There were two other gunshot victims in the emergency room of Northwestern Memorial Hospital when Rell walked Jah in, and the three victims were quickly taken away.

Rell had just sat down between Tamera and Tirzah when his smartphone rang. He had to keep wiping away tears from his eyes as he answered the call.

It was Big Man.

"We ain't gon' be able to make it to Miami, Pops. Jah just got shot."

"Shot? What do you mean?"

"Some niggas tried to rob us at the building. Jah got hit. Just once in the stomach. He should be okay. I'm worried that the bullet might've traveled around in his stomach. It was a small-ass gun. A .25. I took it from the lil nigga."

"Oh, God, please watch over my son. Wrap your arms around my baby boy..."

Rell dropped his head back and listened to his father's heartfelt prayer. The tears came back, and again he wiped them away, telling himself that there was nothing to be concerned about, that Jah was going to be just fine.

He felt Tamera's hand on his shoulder, massaging it. "It'll be okay," she said. "It's just a stomach wound. Nothing to worry too much over. Put it in God's hands."

Rell wasn't sure if the tears he kept wiping away were from the pain he felt for Jah or because he felt he'd let his younger brother down by not protecting him. He wished that he could have jumped in front of the gun and taken the bullet for Jah. Then maybe he wouldn't be feeling so hurt emotionally. He preferred to face physical pain rather than to experience the emotional anguish of seeing Jah in pain.

When Big Man finished praying, he said, "Stay there with your brother. I'll be flying in on the next flight—"

"I got this, Pops," Rell said, cutting his father off. "It's just a stomach wound. He should be fine. I know y'all want this ring. I'll mail it out first thing in the morning."

"Son, I don't give a rat's ass about that ring. As a matter of fact, I don't even want you to send it. Just put it up. Put it back in the bedroom when you get the chance. Susan will just have to wait. Your brother's well-being is of the utmost importance. Damn that ring."

"Let me call you back, Pops."

"Make sure you do."

Putting down the smartphone, Rell leaned over and buried his face in Tamera's lap. Not to cry, but to think. He was more worried than he'd ever been, and he was angry at himself for not killing the teens when he had the chance.

"Everything will be okay," Tamera murmured. Now she was massaging both of his shoulders.

Rell sat up a moment later. He looked around the waiting room, then turned to Tirzah as she spoke.

"I'll stay here with Jah," she said. "I don't think it's a good idea for you to be in here with those guns on you. You know the police will be in here trying to ask questions about how he got shot. You're better off leaving. I'll keep Tamera's car and take him home when he's ready to leave. I got the gun we took from Webb just in case something pops off. You really should go, Rell."

"Yeah, let's go. Call your mom," Tamera said, getting up from her chair. "I'm sure she'll wanna know what's going on with her son."

Reluctantly, Rell took their advice and left with Tamera. She left her car keys with Tirzah, and they took his car.

As soon as Tamera pulled off, Rell dialed his mother's number and shook his head at what was to come. Jah was Momma's baby boy. He had a feeling she was going to lose it.

He reclined the passenger seat as the phone rang in his ear, looking over at Tamera. She was a pretty good driver, a lot better than Erica, who complained about every driver on the road as if they were the source of her driving inabilities.

Momma answered and immediately went in on him: "Where is my motherfucking weed, nigga? I'm sittin' here sober as a preacher. Hell, I could've went and got my own damn sack by now."

"Jah got shot in the stomach." When seconds passed with no reply, Rell continued. "Did you hear me? I said Jah got shot in the stomach. He's at Northwestern. I just dropped him off."

"Who, Rell? Shit. Who shot my baby?"

"Some young niggas. Don't even trip. I'm about to take care of 'em myself. I just wanted to let you know what—"

"You better kill the nigga who did it, you hear me?" She was already crying. "I want his fuckin' brains blown out for this shit. Nobody hurts my baby and gets away with it, Rell. Nobody!"

Rell gave Momma a moment to settle down before he said, "You goin' to the hospital?"

"I'm on my way."

"He's there. Call me when you get there. Love you, Ma."

"Make sure those guys are handled, Rell. I'm as serious as a heart attack. If they shot him they'll shoot you."

"I'm on my way to tend to this situation now, Ma. Just get to the hospital and stay with Jah until I get back. Love you."

He felt compelled to throw the smartphone out his window as the call ended, but instead, gritting his teeth, he put it in his pocket and gave his glove compartment a sharp jab.

He had all three guns—his, Jah's, and the one he'd taken from the robber. The extended clips were in the inside pocket of his jacket. He took them out and loaded them into his and Jah's pistols.

"Don't you think you should be getting rid of those guns?" Tamera said, regarding him with a look of concern. "If you get caught with them and the cops trace them back to those bodies, your ass is going down forever." When he didn't reply she asked, "Where are we going?"

"To the house," he said. "On Trumbull. I gotta find out where to find them lil niggas. Jah told me their names. E, Zo, and Chris."

"Zo lives with his grandmother downstairs from my apartment. Ms. Ida. She's a nice old lady. Originally from Dallas, Texas."

Rell nodded his head. He remembered collecting rent from Ms. Ida and seeing a teenaged boy lying on the living room sofa, but at the time, he'd been too focused on getting the money and hadn't paid much attention to the teen.

"I really want that lil nigga who upped the strap on us. Don't know why I didn't just nail his ass right there when he was knocked out."

"Because you're smarter than that, Rell. And because they were just kids. I saw how swollen that boy's face was, anyway. Looked like he'd had enough. They won't be trying you again."

"Nah, fuck that. A nigga gotta go about my lil bruh gettin' shot."

Tamera sucked her teeth and turned to him as she pulled to a stop at a red light. He kept his attention on the guns on his lap, but out of the corner of his eye he saw her looking at him.

"I'll tell you what," she said, and he could tell that an ultimatum was on the way. "Either we go home and sit down to think about stuff that's more important than killing some stupid-ass kids, or this little thing of ours is over before it's even started. Now, the choice is yours. Let me know right this minute what it's going to be."

He didn't give her an answer.

She took off Susan's diamond ring and dropped it on his lap, right between the two pistols.

Chapter 13

"Feel like a chopper, bitch, cause I'm bussin'
My bitches related, they kissin' cousins
My nina be on that, that bitch ain't for nothin'
I make her say somethin', she leave yo' ass open
I'm bout that combat, right now, I'm strapped
Thirty in forty, t-shirt a shorty
Designer and schemes, my wrist on beam
Hundreds on hundreds, M.U.B.U. abundant
Foreigns back to back, haters have asthma attacks
Pull up, pump a nigga, call it a asthma attack
That 40 cal. always spit, it think it know how to rap
I don't do battle rap, tell 'em to battle that

Pull up, my roof missing, boy, I'll get you missing
Bein' broke as a joke, that's mission impossible
Got hitters to kill a nigga, the streets really feel a nigga
I'm sorry I fucked yo' bitch, but she really dig a nigga
Louie, he B.O.N., bitch, I'm a big ol' nigga
Hope I don't catch a body, ride with my double trigger
I don't like the nigga, fonem pop the nigga
No time to fight the nigga, fonem pop the nigga..."

"Turn down that mu'fuckin' music, nigga!" Zo said. He picked up a dirty spoon off the kitchen table and threw it at his ten-year-old brother Roddy's head.

Roddy ducked out of the way just in time to avoid being hit and took off running out of the kitchen and into his bedroom, where he quickly lowered the music volume on the King Louie mixtape he'd been playing day and night ever since he got it for his birthday last month.

Zo looked across the table at E and Chris. They were all scared for their lives, though no one would admit it. Chris's face was swollen beyond recognition. He had a Ziploc bag full of ice wrapped in a towel, and he was holding it to his face. Jah had given E a black eye. Zo's eye was bruised a little, but not as badly as E's.

"I told yo' dumb ass we needed a real gun, nigga!" Zo snapped at Chris. "But nah, you wanted to pull out that lil bitty-ass .25. Look what the fuck it got us. Not a goddamn thing but some busted-up faces and a real hitta on our asses."

Zo shoved away from the table and walked to the kitchen window. Peeking out through the blinds, he could see the alley behind his sister Odella's house on 15th and Spaulding.

Odella was in her bedroom with Leon, the father of three of her five children. Although Zo usually stayed with Grandma Ida, he was always welcome in his sister's house. Whenever he pulled off a successful robbery, he always came through and blessed her with some of the spoils. She needed it. She was on welfare with no job. Leon didn't have a job, either, and he wasn't much of a hustler.

"We could've got the money, man," E said, shaking his head. "Should've made 'em lay down first. Or made 'em put up they hands. Shit wasn't s'posed to go down like that. Now we gotta be on the lookout for Jah and we didn't even get no bread out the situation."

Zo was heated. "Fuck Jah," he said, and plopped back down in the chair. He took a half cigarette out of the ashtray and fired it up, thinking of a way out of the waist-high shit he and his crew were in.

He watched a roach crawl toward him on the table. It paused at a Dorito crumb, nibbled at it, then turned to face Chris, its antennas swaying in every direction.

Five minutes passed without a single idea as to how he'd deal with Jah. Leon, an out of shape man in his late twenties with nappy hair and a beer belly, came in the kitchen scratching his forearm and looking like he was ready to go to sleep.

"The hell y'all lil niggas in here—" he started, then froze as he caught sight of Chris's brutally beaten face. "Daaaaamn. Who fucked you up?"

"We tried to rob Jah and his puss'-ass brother," Zo said. "They got down on us. Took the strap from Chris and everything. I'm too mad."

"Them niggas over on Millard want Jah's head." Leon opened the refrigerator but kept his eyes on Chris. "I heard one of 'em even got some money on him. Y'all might've been better off just whackin' that nigga and collectin' that bounty." He took a pitcher of tea out of the fridge and poured some right in his mouth.

Zo said, "How much they got on his head?"

"Ten racks. That's what I heard. It's the C's that's at him. They at him and the other Travs off 13th. Shit, y'all better be careful out there in them streets. They say Ray and his cousin Tazz just got hit up on Albany. And some lil girl got killed, too. Shit real out there. They ain't discriminatin'. And them niggas on Millard ain't the only ones at Jah's head. Y'all know Lil Webb. I hear he at Jah and Rell, too. They jumped on Webb the other day. His money too long, so I know he probably got some bread on them niggas, too."

Zo was nodding his head. He smoked the cigarette down to the butt before smashing it out in the ashtray. "Ten racks? I'll whack two niggas for that much money."

"All you gotta do is holla at them niggas on 16th and Millard. They might fuck around and give you a strap to do it with."

"As long as it ain't no punk-ass .25."

"A .25? That's what y'all had?" Leon asked.

Zo pointed a finger at Chris. "That's what his stupid ass had. Swore up and down he was gon' shoot some shit down with it if they didn't run that bread. Ended up gettin' that lil piece o' shit strap took and damn near got us all whacked."

Leon laughed and shook his head all the way back to the bedroom.

"I'ma kill Jah myself," Chris mumbled.

"Shut the fuck up. Yo' bitch ass ain't gon' kill nobody," Zo snapped.

He found another cigarette in the ashtray with a nice amount of tobacco left in it and fired it up. As he smoked, he went back to thinking.

Roddy began playing another King Louie song:

"Smoking dope, riding foreign and, my bitch, she European
Louis luggage on the boat with some coke, you wanna see it?
I'm talking stupid stupid cash, stupid stupid stupid cash
If I told you I was really getting dough, would you believe it?

Bussin' moves at the car lot, front, y'all look like a collar
Got yo' bitch off the molly, off the molly, turnin' up!
Smoke lots of pot, I get ass and top, I get cash a lot
He don't get cash, he just lie a lot, he broke, he lies a lot!
My shoes ain't out, bitch, my jeans ain't out, my outfit, it ain't
out
I'm smoking Ralph, nigga smoking Sway, I told him it ain't
loud!
Smoking def, my pack need a ref, my dick need a rest
Yo' bitch hit the best, two thumbs up for her, she showin' out!
My name is Louie, but they call my Tony, so much money on
me
I ain't lacking, got that nigga on me, so I run up on him
M.U.B.U. now, spread the news around, fuck boy move around
Shooters out, them real shooters out, shoot yo' shooters
down..."

Just as the King Louie song came to an end, Zo thought of
something.
It was a plan to get Jah taken out before he could get to them,
and Zo thought that it was a pretty good plan.

Chapter 14

Rell managed to talk Tamera into putting the ring back on when they returned to his and Jah's new home on 15th and Trumbull. He'd done it while lying across her lap on the sofa, gazing up at her and toying with her right earlobe while she ran her fingernails through his scalp. Now, her left hand was on the chest of his hoodie, and she was staring into his eyes, still scratching gently at his scalp. *The Nightmare Before Christmas* was playing on the muted television. August Alsina was crooning from Tamera's smartphone via her soundcloud app, but neither of them were really listening to the song. Rell was staring up at the ceiling fan, thinking about Jah. Tamera seemed to be thinking about Rell, judging by the loving look in her almond-shaped eyes.

"You are way too fine to be out in the streets being all gangster and shit," she muttered. "You need a good woman in your life, Rell. You need yourself a real, down-ass bitch, and I'm that bitch. Can't wait for the day when you realize that."

"I can see it already." He bit down on his bottom lip. "I wouldn't be laying here if I didn't see it."

"Your ass better see it." She lifted her left hand and studied the ring for a long, silent moment. "I'm telling you, Rell, I've never been with a good man before, and I have high hopes for us. I can see us doing big things together. That's if I'm what you're looking for."

Rell eyed the ring just as closely as Tamera had when her hand made it back down to his chest. Tamera Lyon was definitely what he was looking for. He chuckled as he thought of how quickly she'd rushed to her sister's aid when Webb had grabbed Tirzah by the throat and yanked her out of their apartment.

"What are you laughing at?" she asked.

"Y'all fucked that nigga Webb up."

"He shouldn't have put his hands on my sister."

"Didn't say you was wrong. It was funny, though. She got to crackin' him upside his head with that bat, and you kneed him all in the face. Then he tried to up strap and she knocked him out with the bat. That shit was hilarious."

"Yeah, well, I just hope we don't have to fuck his ass up again. He better just stay the fuck away from us. I don't know why she was givin' him the pussy, anyway. It ain't like he was cashin' out, and he was fuckin' fifty other bitches. I can't deal with a nigga like him. I mean, Kendrick wasn't shit either, but at least he paid all the bills. That nigga Webb didn't do nothin' but give my sister dick and headaches. I was glad to finally kick his ass. You don't know how long I waited for that day to come."

"Fuck that nigga."

Just then, Tamera's phone rang. She looked at it, and her eyes got wide. She ignored the call.

Rell frowned. "Who was that?"

"Nobody."

"I ain't never met a nigga named nobody."

"It was...Kendrick. Calling from prison. He calls me sometimes."

The frown remained. Rell didn't know how to take this. Should he get upset about it, or keep it gangsta and not say a thing?

"He doesn't know about us yet," she said. "That's all it is. I'll let him know."

"Mm hmm." Rell nodded, his upper lip tucked behind his lower one, his eyes squinted in speculation.

Her phone rang again.

Rell sat up. "Go on and talk to him. I gotta piss, anyway," he said, and headed for the bathroom.

Chapter 15

"I know you saw me callin' the first time."

"I did. Was busy doing something. What's up?"

"Busy doin' what?"

Tamera sucked her teeth. "Don't start with me, Kendrick. Today is not the day."

"Look...I need you to do somethin' for me. Need you to go and get me a Vanilla reload card for fifty bucks so I can buy me some squares. I need it by seven o'clock tonight."

"What's a Vanilla card?"

"It's like Greendot. They stopped sellin' Greendots so we use Vanilla reload cards now. Can you do it or not?"

"You gon' send me the money to get it?"

"What? You can't let me get fifty dollars? Take it out that car I bought you."

"I ain't got it. I just had to pay my rent a few days early, and I don't go back to work until the second of January. I can't afford to waste a dime right now."

"Waste? It wasn't a waste when I bought you that car and all that furniture."

"Stop throwing that in my face. If you didn't wanna give it to me, you shouldn't have bought it. I don't have fifty dollars to give you, and that's that."

He went quiet for a moment. Tamera could hear the steady clinking of weights being lifted in the background, along with what sounded like a bouncing basketball and the screeching soles of sneakers on wood. He was in the gym.

"You full of shit, you know that?" Kendrick hissed. "After all the shit I done did for you, you gon' treat me like this?"

"I'm not treating you like anything, Kendrick. Listen, I'm not about to go through this with you. And you can't be calling me no more, either."

"What?"

"I'm with somebody." Tamera said it quickly, hurrying to let it out before she lost the courage.

"Fuck you mean you 'with somebody'? What the fuck is that supposed to mean?"

She sighed. "I got a nigga, Kendrick. A nigga I just met. That's all. I don't wanna disrespect him like that."

"Who? What's his name?"

"I'm not about to tell you that."

"I can't know the name of the nigga who just started fuckin' my wife?"

"Oh, now I'm your wife? If I was your wife, you wouldn't have had two kids by two other hoes when we were together. Don't even play that game. We both know what it was, and I'm not about to keep going through that shit with you."

Tamera was tempted to hang up just then. After being with a real nigga like Rell, she no longer wanted anything to do with Kendrick. As far as she was concerned, he could stay with the mothers of his kids and leave her alone.

"I was really callin' to let you know what my lawyer told me this mornin', but I'm guessin' you ain't tryna hear that, huh?"

"Not really."

"Well, fuck you, then. Bitch, take my mothafuckin' car to my—"

"Nigga, who the fuck are you calling a bitch?! You better watch that shit!"

"Man, fuck you and that hoe-ass nigga! I'm comin' home a lot sooner than you think, bitch. I got somethin' for both of you mutha-fuckas."

"So you're threatening me? Really, Kendrick?" Tamera said, fighting back a wave of tears.

Kendrick hung up without another word.

Slowly, Tamera brought the smartphone down to her side, sneering at its screen. A lone teardrop rolled down from her left eye and clung to her chin. The August Alsina album continued to play from where it had stopped when the phone rang, and she listened to it while she wondered what news Kendrick's lawyer had given him this morning.

Chapter 16

"...It's 2 o'clock and I'm faded, this kush feeling amazing
Got a voicemail on my phone from a lil breezy feeling X-rated
She told a nigga she hurtin', I'm in the car and I'm swervin'
I walked into her bedroom, I put it down that's certain
Man. I stay on that Ciroc, man. I stay takin' shots
Man. your girl be on my jock, maybe because I'm everything
you're not
See I ain't no bitch nigga, no rich nigga, no snitch nigga
I'm a real nigga, that's real nigga - I'm just trying to chill 'cause
I'm way too drunk to be talking like this
I'm way too high to be trippin' like this
I'm way too young to be livin' like this
Ask me why I do it? I'ma put it like this

Goddammit I luv it, I luv it
I luv it, I luv it
Goddammit I luv it, I luv it
Luv it, I luv it
So I'ma keep on drinking 'cause I luv this shit
And Ima keep on smoking 'cause I luv this shit
And I'ma keep on grindin 'cause I luv this shit
She tell me keep fuckin 'cause she luv this shit; and I luv it..."

Rell was standing at the sink, looking at himself in the mirror and nodding his head to the song that was playing from Tamera's smartphone. The music let him know that she was no longer talking to her ex, but Rell didn't want to go back out to the living room just yet.

His mind was on other things.

He phoned Lil Larry, one of Jah's best friends, and told him what had happened to Jah. Then he placed a call to Big Man, but got no answer.

Finally, he phoned Felicia, the mother of Jah's daughter.

"What?" she answered. It was obvious that she was still upset over catching Jah creeping with Tirzah.

"Jah got shot." He said this and waited for Felicia's reaction.

The sound of her gasping in shock made him feel comfortable enough to go on.

"Some lil niggas tried to stick us up. I beat up the nigga who had the gun, but he started shootin' and hit lil bruh. It's just a stomach wound. He should be a'ight. That's what I'm hoping, at least. We took him to Northwestern."

"Oh my God, Rell."

"I know. Crazy."

"Should I go up there?"

"Nah," Rell said, knowing for certain that a fight would break out between Felicia and Tirzah if that were to happen. "He'll probably be out of there within a few hours. I'm just letting you know."

"What was he doing with that bitch Tirzah the other day? Webb said Tirzah fucked Jah. Any truth to that?"

Rell chuckled once.

"Never mind," Felicia said. "Don't even know why I asked you. Like you would tell on your little brother."

"I don't know nothin'."

"Yeah, I just bet you don't."

"Want me to have him call you when he gets home?"

"Of course. Not that I wanna talk to his no-good ass. Once I hear he's okay. I'm cussing his ass out and hanging up."

"You're so mean. Where's my niece?"

"With my sister. Why, you want her? 'Cause I'll drop her lil crying ass right on off to you so we can go out and enjoy ourselves tonight."

"Yeah, bring her to me. I'm on Trumbull. 1530 South Trumbull. It's our new address."

Felicia sucked her teeth and paused; then, "Hold on, did you say Trumbull? Who lives there? I'm not leaving my baby at no stranger's—"

"Big Man got us a house on Trumbull. We ain't really moved all the way in yet. but it's ours."

"So," she probed, "do you mean he's renting it for you and Jah? Or are you saying he actually bought it."

"Rented it." Rell was smiling as the lie fell out of his mouth.

"Bullshit. Big Man is into real estate. I doubt he would rent a house when he owns several of them. He bought it, didn't he? He bought y'all a house. For Christmas, wasn't it? It's a Christmas present."

Rell busted out laughing. Listening to Felicia figure it all out on her own was entertaining. She had always been a smart girl, which is why Maria always said that Jah couldn't have possibly picked a better mother for his kid.

"I hope my baby gets cut in on some of these bands Big Man keeps spending. I need to talk to him."

"What you need to do is stop jumpin' to conclusions. I said he was renting this house for us."

"And I said your ass is lying. I'll be over there in about an hour. You said 1530, right?"

"Yeah. Right around the corner from my daddy's building on Homan."

"Okay, bye, ol' lyin'-ass boy."

The conversation with Felicia lightened Rell's mood. He stopped in the kitchen and grabbed a Pepsi from the refrigerator before walking back out to the living room.

Tamera was sniffling and thumbing tears from her eyes, looking thicker than a Snickers bar in her snug-fitting jeans.

"Why are you crying?" Rell leaned over her and planted a kiss on her forehead. "You good?"

"I'm fine. It's just that I hate being disrespected. Especially by somebody I once loved, you know. It's not a good feeling."

"You told him about me?"

She nodded. "That's what did it. He's pissed. Threatened us and everything."

"We ain't worried about no threats, baby. Get up." Rell put his hands on her ribs and guided her to her feet. Then his hands wandered around to her back and down to her ass. He pushed his fingers down in the back pockets of her jeans and squeezed as he kissed her succulent lips. "We'll be good. Fuck the world. As long as we got each other, nothin' else matters. Fuck dude. He ain't gon' do shit but get beat up worse than y'all did Webb."

His mouth went to her neck, and again he kissed. He felt intoxicated by the fragrance of her perfume. His hands slipped out of the pockets, up her back, and back down to her ass.

His dick grew hard almost instantly.

"I just told you my ex threatened us, and this is what I get? Great." Tamera's tone was replete with sarcasm, but she was undeniably melting under his touch.

The more he kissed and sucked at her neck, the faster her breathing became.

He took a step back, but only long enough to take the guns off his waist and set them on the coffee table. Then he was at it again, this time undressing her as he kissed at the spot that had driven her wild last night.

He was glad when she was finally down to just her bra and panties. He sat her down on the sofa, removed the panties, lifted up her meaty legs, and flickered his tongue across her clitoris. The delicious taste of her pussy made him thirsty for her juices.

He delved his tongue inside of her to quench his thirst, then refocused on her clit and sucked it while ramming two fingers into her tight, juicy tunnel. She palmed the back of his head, freed her breasts from the bra, and pinched her nipples as he tongued her down below.

A long, tight suction on her clitoris was all it took to send her into orgasm. Her legs just about vibrated as she came, gasping and moaning and holding his head in both hands. She begged him to stop and shoved away from him when he didn't comply. She moved to the corner of the sofa, breathing hard, staring at him with a beaming smile.

"You're the pussy-eating champion of the world," she concluded, shutting her legs to keep his shiny wet mouth from attacking.

"Stop runnin'," Rell said, licking the tastiness from his lips.

"Hey, I've got the right to run when I'm in danger. Fight or flight. Didn't you learn about that in school?"

"They didn't teach that in sex ed."

"Well, they should have." Tamera put her hands over her breasts, as if she'd suddenly gotten shy. Her eyes locked onto his belt as he unbuckled it. "Let me see that savage you've got down there."

"Savage?" Rell chuckled.

"Yeah. That fat thing is most definitely a savage."

Rell knew that he was a well-endowed young man, and he was all too proud to open his baggy jeans and unleash the beast.

As soon as he whipped it out, Tamera moved over so that she was in front of him and spread her legs wide apart.

"Look at you," Rell said. "Lil hot ass."

"Shut up and put it in." She wore the guiltiest expression.

Rell did not hesitate.

He prodded in the head, then added an inch, then another two inches, then three more, watching as Tamera's lips curled over her teeth in a look that might have been cause for laughter if he weren't impaling her.

He pushed her knees up and pounded in and out of her with little concern as to how she felt. Her pussy was so unbearably hot and tight, so sopping wet, that he had to pull out just moments later to keep from ejaculating too quickly.

"Mm hmm," Tamera said, smiling. "It's too good, ain't it? Too tight for you."

Rell leaned forward and gave her the juiciest kiss he'd ever given a woman as he sank his pole back into her.

He rubbed her smooth, chocolate legs as he thrust into her. Tamera Lyon was perfect in every way, in Rell's opinion. From head to toe. Rell felt that, with his ruthless past, he didn't deserve such a stunning queen to have all to himself. Nonetheless, he was happy to have her.

August Alsina was still singing his lungs out from Tamera's smartphone. Rell had never listened to August, but right now he appreciated the talented young singer for helping make this moment so special.

"...Baby, I don't blame you
For being in the clubs
And getting all that love
'Cause you're so beautiful
God made you to show that off
Now I ain't ever been the jealous type of guy
But I want you to myself, I can't lie
I know we ain't on no one on one thing
But baby, it should change
'Cause when I be out with other chicks, I be thinking 'bout you
And when you be out on dates you be texting me too
Telling me to come pick you up when he drop you off
I pray to God he ain't breaking you off

I don't want nobody but you
Kissin' on my tattoos
I don't want nobody but me
Talkin' to you
Until you fall asleep
We better stop playing (We better stop playing)
Before we mess around and someone gets hurt
I don't want nobody but you (nobody but you)
Kissin' on my tattoos

Nobody but you
Kissin' on me
Kissin' on me...'

Rell kissed and nibbled at Tamera's lips, basking in the warmth of her until he could no longer take it.

With a sharp gasp, he came.

The orgasmic spasms seemed to last forever.

Chapter 17

Webb had seven staples in the left side of his scalp and three stitches in his left eyebrow. He'd suffered a concussion from the beating Tirzah and Tamera gave him, but he was fine. Nothing major. He'd recovered and returned to the hustle like a boss, cooking up the kilo of coke he'd bought in Georgia into forty-four ounces of crack and having his teenaged dealers sell it in small baggies of $10 and $20 rocks. He also had four ounces of heroin and pints of Promethazine with Codeine for sale.

Losing Tirzah didn't matter much to him, either. Already he had upgraded to Jazzmine, an 18-year-old stripper from Baltimore who was twice as thick as Tirzah and ten times as street savvy. She'd flown here to Chicago on her own dollar, and she had also paid the rental fees for the white Mercedes Benz S550 that she was now driving down Independence Boulevard while Webb sat in the passenger seat and counted through the huge pile of drug money he'd collected from his workers this morning. It was the money his workers had brought in from last night's sales. The cash amounted to $24,750.

"You made all that in one day?" Jazzmine asked, glancing over at him.

Webb nodded his head yes. "Yeah. Why, niggas in Baltimore ain't clockin' like this?"

"Niggas get money everywhere, my nigga, so don't go gettin' a big head about the shit. I was just asking."

Webb could not help but to laugh. Jazzmine was the shit. She had on a long-sleeved white shirt over jeans and black calf-high boots with white fur peeking out at the top. Her fingers glowed with gold and diamond rings. She sported a diamond tennis bracelet with a matching necklace that had a pendant that read "BBBB" in white and yellow diamonds hanging from it.

In the backseat behind Webb sat Lil Zo, one of the youngsters who Webb had been thinking of putting on for a while now. Zo had contacted him a little over an hour ago, and Webb had stopped by Zo's sister's house to pick him up immediately afterward.

"Nah, I make more than this in a day. This is just one night," Webb said. "If you don't mind me asking, what's those four B's for? On your necklace."

"Big Booty Bad Bitches." Jazzmine laughed. "It's a group I started because the skinny bitches at the strip club were hating on us thicker women. There's five of us: me, Buss It, Candy, So Strapped—"

"Don't give me no fuckin' stripper names," Webb interrupted. "You don't call them that shit."

Jazzmine sucked her teeth in a show of indignation. "Okay, asshole." She rolled her eyes, smiling her wonderful smile. "Me, Tela, Nyasia, Crystal, and Marketa. We're the main bitches niggas come to the club to see, and in case you're wondering, yes, they know all about you. And they're waiting to hear how this little trip went when I get back to Bodymore."

"Bodymore? They ain't killin' shit out there."

"Oh, yes the fuck they are. Maybe not like here in Chicago, but it definitely goes down in B-more. Don't sleep on us."

"You should've brought them big booty bitches here with you. Make a left turn up here."

"Brought them with me? For what? I don't do the sharing."

"Sharing is caring, baby."

"If you ever lay a finger on one of my friends I'll fucking kill you, Webb. Seriously. Don't get fucked up."

Grinning, Webb leaned toward Jazzmine and tried to kiss her on the cheek. She bobbed away from him, palmed his face, and shoved it back.

"Get off me, boy."

Webb had a gray leather Gucci backpack resting between his sneakers that he used to carry his money in. He put the cash in it and then leaned back in his seat, eyeing the neighborhood as Jazzmine turned onto 13th and Avers.

"I have got to buy me one of these Benzes one day," Jazzmine said thoughtfully.

"Yeah, it is nice. Park next to this school right here. And keep the car running."

"Webb, if you got me over some bitch's house, I'm fucking you up."

"Just do what the fuck I said."

Jazzmine pulled over and parked behind a green Honda.

Webb sat there for a minute, thinking. He realized that he had not thought this all the way through, that he really didn't even have a plan. He just knew that something had to be done.

He turned to look at Zo in the backseat. "How much it's gon' cost me to get you to air that nigga's crib out for me?"

"I told you, I already don't like the nigga. It's whatever. Just put me on my feet and I'm on it."

Webb nodded and drew a Tec-9 submachine gun from inside the backpack. He heard Jazzmine gasp as he gave it to Zo and pointed at a house across the street.

"Air that mu'fucka out," he said to Zo.

Webb sat back and watched as the kid got out and sprayed the house with bullets.

Chapter 18

"...You ain't talkin' 'bout my niggas then what you talkin' 'bout?
   Gangstas move in silence, nigga, and I don't talk a lot
   I don't say a word, I don't say a word
   Was on my grind and now I got what I deserve, fuck nigga
   Hold up wait a minute, y'all thought I was finished?
   When I bought that Aston Martin y'all thought it was rented?
   Flexin' on these niggas, I'm like Popeye on his spinach
   Double M, yeah that's my team, Rozay the captain, I'm the lieu-
tenant
   I'm the type to count a million cash then grind like I'm broke
   That Lambo my new bitch, but she don't ride like my ghost
   I'm ridin' around my city with my hands strapped on my toast
   'Cause these niggas want me dead and I gotta make it back
home
   'Cause my momma need that bill money and my son need some
milk
   These niggas tryna take my life, they fuck around get killed
   You fuck around, you fuck around, you fuck around, get
smoked
   'Cause these Philly niggas I brought with me don't fuck around,
no joke
   All I know is murder, when it comes to me
   I got young niggas that's rollin' I got niggas throwin' b's
   I done did the DOAs, I done did the KODs
   Every time I'm in that bitch I get to throwin' 30 G's
   Now I'm hanging out that drop head, I'm riding down on Col-
lins
   They let my nigga Ern back home, that young nigga be wildin'
   We young niggas and we mobbin', like Batman I'm with rob-
bin' (Robin)
   This two-door Maybach, with my seat all reclinin'
   I'm like real nigga what up, real nigga what up
   If you ain't about that murder game then pussy nigga shut up..."

"That nigga Meek Mill goes so fuckin' hard, baby!" Rell shouted to Tamera.

She was in the bathtub while he himself was at the living room window with his Beats headphones on, gazing out at the snow-covered Trumbull Avenue and listening to music on his smartphone.

It felt strange knowing that the window he was staring out of actually belonged to him. There would never be a landlord pulling up demanding monthly payments. If he wanted to rent out his apartment, he could do it at any time.

Big Man was the best.

Outside, there were three girls sitting in a smoke-filled van. If not for Tamera being his lady now, Rell thought he might have joined them. Further down Trumbull, four young boys and a man were attempting to build a snowman. They had the biggest ball of snow already done and placed in their yard and now they were working on the midsection. Cars were parked all along the street but no one else was outside.

It was a peaceful winter day on Trumbull Avenue, one of those days that was meant for good times with good people.

Rell had been standing at the window for close to ten minutes when the UPS truck arrived. The sight of it brought a cheerful smile to his face that only broadened as the man got out of the truck carrying his package. He waited for the UPS man to arrive at his doorstep to leave the window for the door.

"Good morning, sir," he said, full of the holiday spirit as he accepted the bouquet of two dozen red roses and the heart-shaped box of chocolates he'd ordered online yesterday evening.

He pushed the headphones down around his neck and strode purposefully to the bathroom with the roses and chocolates in hand, hoping Tamera would be just as happy as he imagined she'd be when gave them to her.

He knocked on the door. "Baby, can I come in?"

"Yeah. I'm just in here relaxing, anyway. Thinking."

Rell turned the knob and entered the bathroom, taking a deep breath as he approached her.

He'd underestimated the level of happiness Tamera would express when he presented her with the roses and chocolates. She started crying and laughing and smiling as soon as she saw them.

"You bought these for me?" she said in utter disbelief.

Nodding his head yes, Rell leaned over the tub and kissed Tamera's lips. "Yeah, baby. You like 'em?"

"Oh, my God, Rell, you don't know how long I've wanted a man to give me red roses. I've told all of my exes just how much I love red roses, but you're the first man to ever give me some."

"Well," Rell said, giving her another kiss, "I'm glad I could be the first. Hopefully I'll be the first for a lot of other shit, too."

"You don't understand, Rell. You literally don't understand. You just gave me so much life with this. Oooh, just wait until I get out of this bathtub."

Rell was laughing as he left the bathroom. He sat down at the dining room table and rolled a blunt, proud of himself for having made his woman so incredibly happy. Sure, he was still pissed over Jah being in the hospital with a bullet to the stomach, but Tamera was making his day better already. The memory of how happy she'd been when he gave her the roses and chocolates would be forever tattooed in his memory.

He put the headphones back on, took his Glock and Jah's Ruger out of his pants and set them on the table.

Just seeing the dangerously long clips sticking out of the gun butts made him feel more comfortable and safe. He knew that even if a gang of niggas came at him right now, he had enough firepower to give them hell.

After all, he couldn't let anything happen to the angel God had sent him a few days ago, the angel who was now soaking in the bathtub.

He sat back in the chair and started smoking the blunt of Kush, his mind drifting from Jah to the CVLs on Millard they were beefing with. A part of him wanted to just head down there to try squashing the issue before it got even more out of hand. He knew that the C's would go just as hard as his own gang would go, but he didn't want any more death to come from this. Too much had happened in the past few days to keep at it. There was nothing to be gained from the senseless violence, all of which had started because of a simple fist-fight between Jah and Stain. Now Jah's best friend D-Lo was dead. Stain was dead. Martez, Jamie, Tazz, and Ray were dead.

And last but not least, an innocent child had lost her life in the crossfire.

It was definitely time to rethink some things.

Rell went to another Meek Mill song and vibed to it while he waited for Tamera come out of the bathroom.

"The money turned me into a monster
The money turned my noodles into pasta
The money turned my tuna into lobster
They want to do me I maneuver like a mobster

4 A.M. I'm on the north side of Philly
Riding around like these haters don't want to kill me
It's a shame how they hate on me you gotta feel me
I started out with a dollar and got a milli
I'm like do it for the gram ho, do it for the gram ho
She don't want to bust it I say do it for them bands yo
I say do it for them bands fucking with that broke nigga you should do it for your man
Lately I've been on the low with a ho that you probably know
Took her to the crib and met Momma right at the door
Momma started smiling like Momma I got to go
I done took so many trophies to Momma my momma know
I said a real nigga, I get that money pay them bills nigga
My momma told me, "You a real nigga."
And I be hanging with them real killers
Now what a feeling when you looking at the latest whip and knowing you can cop it
Or looking at the baddest bitch and knowing you could pop it
The youngest nigga in my city doing it, I got it

68

On another level with Benjamin and money is the topic Lord..."

Rell's phone rang just as Tamera came sauntering out of the bathroom. The caller was Johnny B, Jah's friend.

"Lord, you ain't gon' believe this shit, joe," Johnny B said. "A nigga done shot up your mom's house."

Rell's heart dropped to his stomach.

"Niggas saw a white Benz speedin' off," Johnny B continued. "Luckily, your mom wasn't in there. We don't know nobody with a white Benz but we'll be on it, bruh. If we see it 'round this way again, I'm gon' personally flip that bitch, on Neal."

"Yup." It was all Rell could say through his clenched teeth.

Tamera frowned and shook her head from left to right as he ended the call.

"Oh, Lord," she said. "What's happened now?"

Chapter 19

It had taken her more than an hour of begging and pleading, but eventually Susan managed to coax Big Man into going to check out some houses in the Miami area. They wouldn't be using the real estate agent today, but they would in the future, if they found something they agreed on.

Susan couldn't complain. She was merely setting up an opportunity to see the real estate agent again. This time it would just be her and Big Man. Then it would be her, Big Man, and Chuck Calloway, and eventually, when Big Man grew tired of traveling from house to house, it would be just her and Chuck. She had her mind set on a one-night stand whenever that day came.

Since Big Man claimed that the price of living in a nice home in Miami was far too expensive for his wallet, Susan found an appealing home for sale in the nearby suburb of Cutler Bay, Florida. Big Man made the drive south, while Susan swiped through photos of the home on her smartphone and offered him the details.

The photographs gave no justice to the actual house.

Susan's mouth fell open when Big Man pulled up to the three-car garage at 19506 Southwest 78 Place. He parked next to an Altima and shut off the engine.

It was a two-story yellow concrete block stucco home, with an impeccably mowed lawn, an outdoor swimming pool, and a beautiful garden. The house was surrounded by neatly trimmed bushes.

"This is totally worth the $600,000 asking price," Susan said as they got out and headed for the front door.

"Bullshit it is. They better cut us some kind of deal. I'm not paying six hundred grand for this place."

"No, just the twenty-percent down payment. A hundred and twenty grand. I need this space, Dave. Look at the front yard. Look at the garage and all the privacy we'd have. This is perfect for us. I'm not going back to that measly little apartment."

Big Man waved her off as they walked inside. Today the seller was having an open house, and there was also a second, younger Hispanic couple here to look at the home.

Susan could not hold in her excitement. Walking through the house, she gawked at every detail.

Five bedrooms and four bathrooms. 4,967 square feet of living space. A laundry room with a washer and dryer. A dishwasher. An electric range and oven. A breakfast bar and a kitchen island. Secondary bedrooms split from the master bedroom. Tub and separate shower. Walk-in closets.

Susan was instantly in love. Big Man didn't seem so excited about it.

"You are one big cheapskate, you know that?" Susan said as they ventured out to the backyard. "I'm gonna start calling you El Cheapo. With your cheap ass."

"Call me whatever you wanna, but what you won't call me is a fool with my money."

"It's not your money, David; it's ours. Mine and yours." It was Susan's turn to do the waving off. "I know you're mad about what's going on with Jah, but don't take it out on me. I didn't shoot him. I told you Chicago was nothing but trouble, and now look at what's happened. Right after I tell you we shouldn't be living in that hell-hole, your son gets shot during an armed robbery. Seems to me like you might wanna take your wife's advice on this one. I'm not as stupid as you think I am."

"I didn't say you were stupid, Susan. Give me some time to think, alright? Is that too much to ask? My son's in the hospital with a hole in his stomach, and here I am in south Florida looking at a house."

"To keep your family safe."

"Whatever, Susan."

"Listen, David. I understand that you're going through it right now. That's why I'm not going to bug you about my ring today. But tomorrow, if Rell isn't too busy, it would be highly appreciated if you convinced him to go out and put it in the mail."

"Damn that ring."

"Damn you," Susan retorted as she walked away from him to explore the backyard on her own.

Big Man remained in a grumpy mood from then until they made it back to their hotel suite in Miami an hour and a half later, and the only reason the mood ended was because he took a nap.

As soon as he began snoring, Susan took the key to their rented Bentley and headed out the door.

Chapter 20

"...My cousin CJ tried to hit me with a brick of raw
In Alexandria, it's nothing for to get it gone
With music, I ain't won awards, but I kept it gangster
Gone be a God in New Orleans like that nigga Daymond
Landlord in the south like my nigga Luchie
Corvette in front of David Ways screeching free Lee Lucas
Fuck that nigga bitch, I got her saying free Lee Lucas
Beeto and Bryan bitch, I just got off the phone with 'em
My old friends hating, sending me the wrong signals
My dawg recorded conversations, man what's wrong with him?
You got them college niggas fool, I be with stone killers
Doing bad 'fore they switched on me
When you're out of power it's over
Everybody love you when you feed the streets
When you leave the streets, they don't know you
Brook used to love me till another nigga with a bigger check approached her
Up in DCI, when I was calling home she was at the nigga house smoking
I was trying to go to church as a family, but her and him be going
Audi S7 was a surprise, I had went and bought that for her
Texting, saying someone that I love let her use his whip as a loaner
Praise be to God, everything done in the dark really come back on you
Cocaine flipper, got the same niggas I came with, and we rolling
In the studio with my nigga Hood, but them niggas round him, they pussy
Gangster shit, get to going platinum, they'll sit around and be looking
I'm so depressed I'll kill myself, wish somebody go head and cook me
Fuck!

Bet a lot pussy niggas want to murder Brasi
Boulevard, Murcielago and a Maserati
Boobie Black, Gunna, and Menace still a catch a body
And if you fuck around with Rayzor, bitch, I'm out my body
Sideways, coupe be out my body
Whole clique pull up in Vettes, bitch we out our body
And you ever disrespect it then it's kamikaze
I just be with me a shooter like I'm John Gotti
I feel like John Gotti
John Gotti
'Cause it ain't shit to send a hit, I feel like John Gotti
It ain't shit to send a hit, I feel like John Gotti..."

Kevin Gates was Rell's favorite rapper, and usually he turnt up when listening to a Gates song, but now it only served to make him even more alert than he already was.

Sitting in the passenger seat of his Impala while Tamera drove it all throughout the North Lawndale neighborhood, with the Glock and Ruger pistols on his lap and a fiery hatred in his eyes, he was nowhere near turnt up over the "John Gotti" song. If anything, he was turned down.

Tamera knew that he was steaming hot. This time she hadn't questioned him for wanting to go out and search for his enemies. This time she'd quietly put on her clothes and left out the door at his side.

She had driven by Maria's house first, at his request. Seeing the bullet-riddled front door and windows made Rell's chest expand with a breath of anger.

"A'ight," he'd said, nodding his head and gritting his teeth. "A'ight. That's what niggas on? Drive-bys? A'ight. I'm on that."

Now they were on 16th Street. Johnny B and two more young hitters were behind them in a gray Jeep.

"Slide down on Millard," Rell said as he unintentionally glanced at the diamond ring on Tamera's finger.

It occurred to him then that getting married in the future might not be such a bad idea. It would be good to have a real woman to stand by his side during times like this. He hoped that times like this would be rare, but still...there was nothing like a partner who had a man's back through thick and thin.

"They got me ready to shoot somebody out here," she said.

Rell shook his head. "You just drive. Let me handle the shooting."

"That's some real coward shit they did to your mom's house. I mean, who does that? That's not gangster. A real nigga would've waited to catch you in person, not shoot up your momma's house like a little bitch boy. That's some shit a kid would do."

Rell squinted thoughtfully. Maybe Tamera was on to something.

"That's probably what the fuck it was, too," he said. "A kid. One of the lil niggas who tried to rob me."

"You don't know where to find them? We might need to go to the building and check Zo's grandma's apartment. He lives there with her."

"Yeah, slide over there. And if I start blowin', just be ready to speed off when I say go."

"I know where his sister lives, too. We'll check there if he's not at the building."

Rell nodded. Picking up his smartphone, he sent Felicia a text message letting her know what had happened to Momma's house and that she couldn't bring his niece over. She texted back a bunch of angry emojis. Rell ignored the message and phoned Momma.

"You heard what happened to the house?" he said when she answered.

"Of course I heard, Rell." She was sobbing. "What in the world is going on?! Thank God I'm at this hospital. For Christ's sake, it's the end of fucking December! Ain't it too damn cold for this mess? And let me guess: nobody knows who shot up my house, huh? Nobody fucking seen a thing."

"I'm on it, Ma. I'm sorry you gotta go through this shit. You better believe that when I catch up with whoever did it, I'm canceling their new year. The nigga ain't gon' live to see 2016."

Johnny B had given Rell a ski-mask, which he now had rolled up to his forehead. He put the smartphone in his pocket and fixed his eyes on the street ahead.

He wasn't a hundred percent sure whether the people responsible for shooting up his mom's house were the CVLs Jah was beefing with on Millard or the kids who'd attempted to rob him and Jah in their father's apartment building. Hell, for all he knew, it could have even been Webb. After all, he and Jah had been there when the girls beat Webb senseless in the hallway outside of their apartment. Maybe Webb was taking it out on them for being there with Tirzah, who'd been one of Webb's girlfriends at the time.

He doubted if the latter possibility was true but since he didn't know for certain, he kept it in mind.

As Tamera turned onto Homan, the guessing game that was going on in Rell's head came to an end.

He saw it from a block away, parked near the corner on 15th Street, smoke from the exhaust system billowing from its rear pipes.

It was a white Mercedes Benz.

Chapter 21

"Just drive, baby. Drive past real slow, a'ight? Don't get nervous. Speed off when I say go, make a left on 15ᵗʰ, and then another left on Trumbull. We'll be right back at home. Then all you'll have to do is pull into the garage and we'll be good. You got that?" Tamera nodded her head. She looked afraid. Her fingers tightened around the steering wheel. Her eyes darted from the rearview mirror to the sideview mirror and back to the road. She turned off the music and sighed.

Taking a deep breath, Rell lowered his window and waited for her to reach the Mercedes. There were a dozen other vehicles driving up and down Homan. He thought of the little girl Jah had accidentally shot on Albany, which made him look around to make sure that no kids were in the line of fire.

Just as he was sticking his head out of the window with both guns in hand, a police car turned onto Homan from off Douglas.

"Shit." Rell sat back down.

"That's a cop," Tamera said, stating the obvious.

"Just turn onto 15ᵗʰ. We'll circle the block and come right back," Rell said.

He studied the Benz as Tamera made the turn. There was a girl in the driver's seat. No one else.

"You see that bitch right there? Ever seen her before?" he asked Tamera.

"No, I don't think so. But damn her. We need to see who she's sitting there waiting on. I'm willing to bet that it's the guy or guys who shot up your mom's house."

"I know. Pull into this alley right here." He pointed to the alleyway between Homan and Trumbull. "I'm about to find out who they are. Don't even trip. And when I do, it's ugly for 'em."

She crept into the alley, followed by Johnny B in the Jeep.

"Be careful, bae. Gimme a kiss," Tamera said.

Rell did as she asked, and for one magical moment he shut his eyes as their lips connected, inhaling through his nose her alluring scent and praying to God that he would make it out of all this drama alive.

If he did, who knew? He might just end up putting a ring on her finger.

He pushed open his door and got out of the car, putting the guns in his hoodie's belly pocket as Johnny B approached holding an AK-47.

"That's the car," Johnny B said, speaking from behind a face full of dreadlocks. "Ain't nobody else around this mu'fucka got no white Benz. What we on?"

"Nigga, you know what we on." Rell turned and looked at the rear of the house that the Mercedes was parked in front of. "I would just run off in this crib right here, but I ain't sure which house the nigga went in. We'll lay low in the cut right next to this mu'fucka. Whoever we catch walking out to that Benz..."

He didn't finish the sentence, because there was no need to. It went without saying. Johnny B and his two hitters knew exactly why they were here, and Rell knew that they would not hesitate to start squeezing their triggers.

Chapter 22

Zo couldn't believe his luck.

This morning when he woke up he had been so broke that he stole a dollar out of his grandma's purse.

Now, though, he was richer than he'd ever been. Cleaner, too. After he'd shot up Rell and Jah's house on Avers, Webb took him to the mall and bought him a leather Pelle jacket, four whole Robin's Jean outfits, three True Religion outfits, four pairs of Jordans, and a gold chain. Webb had also given him $3,500 in cash, which was now burning a hole in his pocket as he stood at the open basement door, peering down the creaky wood stairs.

Webb had gone down to the basement with Chino, a man who Zo didn't know too well. Zo suspected it was a drug deal. He'd seen Chino around the neighborhood, but had never talked to him. He knew that Chino was a dope boy like Webb, though not nearly as rich. Chino didn't even have a car, and Chino's girlfriend was nowhere near as bad as the girl Webb had waiting out in the Benz.

Zo had bought himself a prepaid smartphone while they were out shopping. He walked into the kitchen, holding his jeans, where the Tec was tucked away. He dialed Chris's mobile number, but only because E didn't have a phone. As expected, E answered.

"Lord, I got some shit to tell y'all niggas, man," Zo said, looking around the kitchen. "I'm on, bruh. I mean on for real. Bands. That nigga Webb hit my hand heavy, joe. I shot up Jah n'em crib on 13ᵗʰ. Fired that mu'fucka up."

"That's what's up, bruh. Did you hit that nigga?"

"Fuck if I know. I know I shot the shit outta his OG crib. With the Tec. The nigga gave me a Tec! Man, I ain't even worried about Jah no more. This Tec gon' end all that tough shit. We can shoot it out broad day. You know I'm wit' it."

"Where you at? We at my crib."

"I'm on Homan, at Chino's spot. Man, you gotta see this bad bitch Webb got."

"The bitch who was in the Benz he picked you up in?"

"Yup. On God, she cold, bruh. She a stripper from somewhere else. Bitch took a plane here. She probably got bread like Webb. But look, when I get back, we gon' get us some weed to sell, bruh. For ourselves, too. I'm done tryna work for niggas. We need to start eatin' like Webb. I'ma ask him to teach me the game. I think he rockin' wit' us now that I done did some shit for him. I might end up being his security. I don't know yet. I'll hit you back when he about to drop me off."

"Yup. Neal."

"Neal." Zo hit end and smiled. He went back to the basement door just as Chino came walking up the stairs ahead of Webb.

The Gucci backpack that Webb had stuffed full of cash in the car was on his shoulder, and Zo found himself wondering how much money was in it. Probably a lot more than the $3,500 Zo had in his pocket.

"Yeah, the bitch hit me with a baseball bat," Webb was saying to Chino. "I caught the bitch fuckin' with the lil nigga Jah. You know Jah. Rell lil brotha. The lil nigga was fuckin' my bitch. I couldn't believe it. When I snatched the hoe up she got to hittin' me with the bat, then they jumped me. Her, her sister, Jah, and Rell. I'm on they ass now. Let me catch 'em in traffic. I just had my lil nigga right here put a thirty in they momma's house to show 'em what it really is. Niggas must've forgot about me. Niggas must've forgot who the fuck I am..."

Zo frowned as he followed them to the front door. He didn't appreciate the fact that Webb was already telling someone about him shooting up the house on 13th and Avers. They didn't even know if he'd shot somebody or not.

He shook his head. They made it to the door, and Chino opened it.

"I'll be at'chu tomorrow," Chino said as he shook Webb's hand.

Webb started off down the stairs.

Zo was on his way out the door behind Webb when Chino put a hand on his shoulder and said, "So, you ain't no game, huh? I didn't know yo' lil ass was out here slangin pistols."

Zo shrugged, looking up at the tall man. "It's just a part of life around here, ain't it? I was born in this shit, and more than likely I'ma die in it. But I'ma be a mu'fucka until that day—"

Zo's eyes went wide as he witnessed four masked men come running out from beside Chino's house, two of them aiming assault rifles at Webb, the other two aiming handguns.

One of them turned and pointed two guns right at Zo and Chino.

Zo ducked and ran back into the house as the bullets started flying.

Chapter 23

Rell was surprised to see that Webb and one of the kids who'd robbed him were together, but he had no time to think it over.

He and the other guys shot Webb more than a dozen times in just a few seconds, then he turned his guns back on the kid and the man who were standing in the doorway on the porch.

The kid was fast. He vanished quickly, but the man fell just inside the door as Rell and Johnny B sent round after round his way.

Rell was tempted to run inside after the boy, but when he remembered that a cop car had driven by this very spot less than two minutes prior he thought better of it. After glancing at Webb to make sure that he was dead (and indeed Webb was as dead as can be, lying disproportionately in the blood-spattered snow with numerous holes in his head and torso) Rell took off running back to the car.

He saw pure fear in Tamera's eyes as she waited for him to get in. As soon as his butt touched the passenger seat she sped off across the vacant lot that led to Trumbull, not even bothering to use the street, while Johnny B and the gang raced away down the alley in their Jeep.

Rell's heart felt like it was going to explode in his chest. Before the shooting he'd been fearless. Now he was more paranoid than ever, hoping that Tamera would make it to his house before another cop car appeared.

"What was his name again? The one who lives with his grandma in my daddy's building?" Rell asked Tamera.

She ignored him as she sped across yet another vacant lot, the one that was next to 1530 South Trumbull Avenue. She came rumbling to a stop right at the garage door, which is when Rell realized that he had yet to even look at the garage, let alone figure out how to open it.

Lucky for him, he wouldn't need to, because the garage door was already raised a couple of inches off the ground. He rushed out of the car and just about threw the door up to the ceiling. Tamera whipped right in, and Rell yanked the door back down.

They went in the house through the back door that led into the kitchen. Rell immediately locked the door behind them. Neither of them bothered to kick loose the snow that was caked on the bottom of their shoes. Rell sat down at the kitchen table while Tamera paced back and forth with her arms folded over her chest.

"Zo. That was his name, right?" Rell said, dropping his head back and rubbing his hands down his face. "The lil nigga who lives with his grandma."

Tamera only nodded.

Seconds later, they both froze at the sound of police sirens. Tamera's eyes and mouth went agape.

Rell hopped up and ran to the bathroom. He had no idea why he'd chosen the bathroom, but it seemed like a good choice at the time. Once there, he frantically scanned every corner of it until he settled on the toilet. He went to the toilet, lifted the tank cover, and dropped the two pistols down into the water before returning the tank cover to its place.

Tamera walked in looking scared out of her mind.

"Rell, can we please go to bed? Just to lie down. I want— no, I need you to hold me."

"Come on," Rell said.

They left their shoes at the foot of the bed and got under the covers. Rell lay on his back. Tamera rested her face on his shoulder and threw a leg over him.

For a few minutes, neither of them spoke. With the television off, the room was silent. Silent and cool; Tamera had shut off the heat before they left out.

Just as Rell realized that he was still wearing the ski-mask, Tamera said, "Take that off. Please. I don't like seeing you in it."

He pushed it up to his forehead and let out a heavy breath.

"Did you get him?" she asked.

Rell nodded his head yes. "That lil nigga Zo got away, though. Well, I think he got away. He might've got hit up when he was running through the house. But Webb's out the game."

"Oh, my God, it was Webb in the Benz? Wait until I tell Tirz."

"Yeah. He got hit good, too. He's done for. Shit. Damn, I hope nobody saw my car back there."

"I didn't see anybody."

"Just because we ain't see nobody don't mean they didn't see us."

"I know." She shivered against him. "We should take your daddy up on that vacation offer. Now's the best time to go."

"Nuh uh. Not while my lil brother's in the hospital."

Tamera sighed. She put her hand on his chest, and they both stared at the diamond ring for a moment.

Images of gunfire and snow kept flashing in Rell's head as he studied the ring. He regretted not shooting Zo when he'd first come from around the side of the house and saw him standing there in the doorway.

"This kind of lifestyle can't continue, Rell." Tamera spoke softly. "I want a family one day. I want to live long, with a good husband, like my granny did until she passed away. My granddaddy died like two weeks after she did. They were together for sixty years. I want something like that, and I'm not going to get it living like this."

Rell took some time to ponder his reply. "That's what I want, too," he said finally. "That's definitely what I want. I'm not on that shit. Niggas are forcing me to do this shit. I didn't ask a nigga to shoot up my momma's house. Webb got what he deserved."

"I agree, but it still has to stop. Okay, he's out of the way, but there's still the issue with those guys on Millard, and the boys who tried robbing you and Jah. It'll never stop unless we stop it ourselves. We have to, Rell. Either that or you're going to eventually end up dead or in jail. Is that what you want?"

"Don't ask me no shit like that."

"The truth hurts, doesn't it? You don't wanna think about that."

Rell was about to reply when the sound of more approaching police sirens silenced him. He rubbed Tamera's shoulder and held her tight against him, eyeing the white diamond engagement ring and wondering when he'd be getting another call from Big Man about it.

Chapter 24

Zo was so scared that he was crying.

Trying his absolute hardest to walk at a normal pace, he was strolling down 16th Street with his head down and a bloody gray leather Gucci backpack strapped over one shoulder. Police cars were zipping past, en route to where Webb and Chino's bullet-riddled bodies were stretched out on 15th and Homan.

The cold air had his nose numb. The Tec-9 was scratching his inner thigh, but he wasn't going to reach down in his pants to readjust it.

Tangela, a 17-year-old girl he'd went to school with last year, walked past him with her mother. She hardly ever noticed him in school but she looked at him now, and he knew that it was because of his fresh outfit and Gucci backpack.

He hoped that she wouldn't notice the blood on it.

When the shooting had begun, he'd sprinted to the rear of the house, only to find that Rell's car was parked in the alley when he looked out the kitchen window. He'd stayed in the kitchen until he saw the masked men running into the alley. Then he ran out the front door.

Upon the discovery of Webb's dead body, he had wasted no time in relieving Webb of the backpack before running off up Homan. Jazzmine had already sped off.

Thinking of her, he looked around, hoping to see the pearly white Mercedes, but he had no such luck. The girl was probably already on her way to the airport to fly back to Baltimore, and more than likely she wouldn't be returning to Chiraq anytime soon. Chicago was too much for most people. He didn't blame her if she never came back.

He kept his eyes peeled for Rell's white Impala and the gray Jeep he'd seen parked behind it in the alley. He tried to guess how many rounds he had left in the Tec, just in case Rell happened to pull down on him. He remembered hearing Webb tell Chino that he'd had his lil guy send thirty shots at the house on Avers, so it had to be at least a 30-round clip. Zo was certain that he had let off no more than a dozen shots. Probably had eighteen rounds or so left.

The one thing Zo was anxious to do was get somewhere alone to count up the money in the backpack. He couldn't go to Granny's apartment, not after what had gone down there with the failed robbery. But he had an even better option. He knew the perfect place to count the money without interruption.

He turned onto Spaulding and took off running to his sister's house. When he got there, he went around back to the rusty old Cadillac that had been in the backyard for years now. He had no idea who the car belonged to, but he and his friends always sat in it to smoke their weed and cigarettes. Usually he demanded that the driver's seat be his throne but this time, alone with the backpack, he went straight for the backseat.

There were two bullet holes in the backpack. He noticed them as he unzipped it and reached inside.

The first thing he felt was plastic. He pulled it out and saw that it was a bag full of a rocky tan-colored substance, then turned the backpack upside down and dumped its contents out on the seat next to him.

What came falling out was more cash than he'd ever seen in his life, along with a second bag of the same kind of rocky brownish substance. He couldn't tell whether the bags were full of crack or heroin, but either way, he was happy.

It took him more than thirty minutes to count the cash. He could have finished sooner if he wasn't so nervous, and if the incessant yell of police sirens didn't keep throwing him off, and if he didn't insist on counting it again to be sure that he hadn't miscounted.

The final count was $29,230.

With the money in his pocket, that was $32,730.

After he put the cash back in the backpack and zipped it shut, he punched the back of the dusty old driver's seat a good fifty times, and yet the joy remained.

"I'm mothafuckin' rich!" he shouted.

Chapter 25

Susan sat in the car for over twenty minutes with the visor mirror down when she made it to the Grove Isle Hotel & Spa, examining her deep red lipstick, putting on eyeliner and eye shadow, fixing her hair into a neat, modest bun. She was wearing the yellow diamond tennis bracelet, earrings, and necklace set that Big Man had bought for her yesterday during a brief shopping spree at Macy's. She'd gotten a text from Chuck saying that he was waiting for her in a suite on the second floor, but she was not about to show up looking a mess. Not to the first date she'd ever had since her and Big Man tied the knot.

She checked her smartphone and dropped it in her purse before stepping out of the sleek Bentley coupe and handing her key to the valet parking employee.

Sauntering through the hotel lobby, heart beating like an African drum, she almost turned around and fled. In all her years on earth she had never been the kind of woman to step out on her man. She'd always looked down on those kinds of women. Her mother had called them "hussies". They were trifling, despicable examples of what a woman should be.

But lately, Susan was feeling differently. Big Man was a boring old fucker with little care for the good life. He wasn't a huge fan of toothpaste, despised traveling, hated spending their hard-earned money in such a way that he was practically an extreme cheapskate, and to top it all off, he was a horrible lay. Susan was getting old, and the last thing she wanted to do was spend her remaining days in a cramped apartment in the coldest city ever with a fat old man who rarely made love to her.

The thought of such a drab, depressing ending compelled Susan to push on toward the elevators.

When she made it to the second floor, she sent Mr. Calloway a text message letting him know that she was here, and a moment later, he poked his head out of a door halfway down the hall and waved for her to join him.

She took a nervous breath and mumbled, "Lord, forgive me," as she walked to him.

Chuck had a fluffy white robe draped over his lean frame. He gave her a warm hug and then pulled back, displaying a glistening Colgate smile. He looked even more handsome than he had earlier. His hair was damp. His only accessory was a gold Rolex watch. He smelled like the Old Spice cologne Big Man used to wear.

"Well, well, well," he said, "aren't you looking like the queen who stole the king's heart."

"Don't be silly."

"I'm not being silly. You're the most beautiful woman I've had the pleasure of meeting in a long while. I really mean that."

The feel of the stranger's eyes on her skin made Susan nervous. He led her to a white leather sofa, fixed two glasses of vodka, and slid one across the table to her.

"There you go. Drink up. Loosen up. We'll head down the hall and get ourselves a spa treatment."

Reluctantly, she took the drink and sipped from it. "My husband can't find out about this. He'd kill me."

"Your secret's safe with me." He drank from his glass, lifted her hand in his, and gave it a gentle kiss. He eyed her bracelet. "Nice. Yellow diamonds. I bought my ex-wife one of these a while back. It's from the Effy collection, am I right? You get it from Macy's?"

Susan smiled and gave a nod. "Four grand for this bracelet. Four more for the earrings and necklace."

"They look good on you."

"Thanks."

"Where are you from, if you don't mind me asking?"

This was the perfect question. Especially with Susan drinking the vodka. She opened right up to him, telling him everything from her childhood on up to her present day circumstances. She even went so far as to give him the details of the marriage that, quite frankly, she no longer wanted.

Chuck opened up to her, as well. He was born and raised in a small town in Connecticut, moved to New York to study law, and then off to Miami Beach he went with a beautiful young blonde who'd cheated on him just weeks into their marriage with the best man. He'd found a second wife in Rebecca Stewart, but she'd also had an itch that he apparently could not scratch, which led to his second divorce. He'd initially been a criminal defense attorney, but had quickly grown tired of seeing minorities being paraded through the prison system. When his father was taken out by lung cancer in 2004 and left him with the real estate company, he abandoned the courtroom for the housing market and hadn't looked back since. Now he lived in Miami Beach in a million-dollar condo with Max, his golden retriever.

"Sounds to me like you're living the high life, Chuck." Susan was on her second drink. The buzz was real. "What about me interests you so much? You ever dated a Black woman?"

A smirk grew on his face. "Not exactly."

"And what does that mean?"

"I had sex with a Black girl a couple of times in high school. She had a boyfriend. We used to do it under the bleachers. Best sex I've ever had. I looked her up a few years ago. She's a child therapist in Saginaw, Michigan, married with kids. Still as beautiful as she was back then."

"Hmm." Susan ran the tip of her index fingernail from Chuck's knee up to the middle of his though, pushing up the robe in the process. There was maybe an inch of hair on his legs. They were strong and toned.

The sight of them turned Susan on.

She balled the collar of his robe in a fist and pulled him to her for a kiss.

Chapter 26

Rell awoke to the sound of someone knocking at the front door.

He reached over to the nightstand, took his smartphone off the charger, and saw that it was a quarter past eight.

Asleep next to him, Tamera looked like a chocolate angel. He pressed his lips on her cheek and got up.

The memory of Webb's dead body came to him immediately. Now that it was dark out, he felt safe from the threat of an arrest for the shooting, yet wary of a possible retaliation. With the kind of money Webb had, someone had to be upset over his death.

He hoped that no one would be able to tie him to Webb's murder.

The knock came again. Three hard knocks at the front door.

Rell stepped into his boots and went to the bathroom. Second later he came out holding the Glock in his right hand, water dripping out of its every crevice. He put it in the back of his jeans when he looked out the living room window and saw who was at the door.

It was Apple. Bundled up in a heavy green coat with a pack of Backwoods cigarillos in one hand and a plastic bag in the other.

Yawning and stretching, Rell went to the door and opened it.

"Damn, you was asleep?" Apple said as he walked in.

"Nah, I was asleep," Rell said sarcastically. "Be quiet, too. Baby in there asleep."

"Baby? Who, Tamera? Nigga, I thought you was wit' Erica?"

"Don't worry about who the fuck I'm with." Rell stuck his head out the door and looked up and down Trumbull before shutting and locking it.

Apple raised his hands in surrender as they went to the dining room table and sat down. "A'ight, killa. You know my fat ass don't want no smoke. Not with the way these lil niggas around here whackin' shit. I just wanna smoke my weed, eat my Italian beefs, and drink, and not necessarily in that order 'cause these sandwiches gotta get it first."

From the plastic bag, Apple took out a Styrofoam tray, some napkins, a can of grape Crush soda pop, and a fifth of Remy Martin that looked like it had just been taken out of the freezer.

Rell's mouth began to water as soon as Apple flipped open the tray lid. There were two steaming hot Italian beef sandwiches stacked up beside a serving of French fries.

"Let me get one of those," Rell said.

Apple scoffed at the request as he shrugged out of his coat. "You can get a piece, nigga. That's about it. You better drive down there and get you one. I just walked twelve blocks to get these sandwiches. Shit, I gotta eat 'em to gain back the weight I lost from that long-ass walk."

"What weight you done lost?" Rell drew back the side of his mouth in a show of disbelief.

"I'll tell you about a loss. Webb and Chino. Them two niggas is lost like a muthafucka. I know you heard all them gunshots earlier."

"Nah, I was asleep with baby," Rell lied.

"Maaaan, somebody tore into them niggas so bad they say the ambulance had to connect the body parts. I heard they hit that nigga Webb so many times his head got found across the street somewhere. Chino was right in his doorway when he got hit up. What's that, like, eight bodies in four days? D-Lo, Stain, Martez, Jamie, Ray and ol' boy on Albany, Webb, and Chino?" He was counting them on his chubby fingers. "Yup, eight damn bodies." He shook his head and reached across the table to Rell with a sandwich in his hand. "Tear you off a piece."

"Ol' petty-ass nigga." Rell tore off as much as he could, and received a cold-eyed stare for the transgression.

"I'll fuck a nigga up about my food," Apple threatened.

Rell chuckled and checked his smartphone as he bit into the sandwich. He had a missed call from Momma and a text message from Jah's phone. He read Jah's message first:

"I'm guwop bruh it wuz thru n thru dat's wut da dr said Tirzah gon bring me home in a lil bit"

Rell breathed a sigh of relief. He'd been worried about Jah's condition and knowing that things were going to be okay was a welcoming feeling.

Instead of returning Momma's call, he sent her a text:

"Yo wussup ma?"

He put the phone down on the table and stuffed the rest of the cheesy sandwich in his mouth while he waited on a reply.

"Get some...cups," Apple said with a mouthful of beef. "And roll up. Know you got some more loud. I want in."

Rell got up and walked around the table, headed for the kitchen. He snapped a hand into the Styrofoam tray as he passed behind Apple and took a handful of fries.

"Muthafucka!" Apple slammed the lid shut and glowered over his shoulder at Rell. "See, that right there is the reason I eat at home. Can't bring no food around niggas. Niggas think shit is automatically theirs, too."

"It is, nigga. That Kush costs money."

"I'll buy my own sack."

"Shut that bullshit up, nigga. Ain't nobody got the same Kush we got, and you know it. That's why yo' fat ass came over here." Rell took two plastic cups out of the cabinet next to the refrigerator and returned to the dining room.

"You ain't lyin'," Apple said, practically laying on top of his tray to keep Rell's hand out of it. "Them niggas down the way ain't got no good shit like y'all do. I was so mu'fuckin' high earlier, man. I went in the house, ate damn near everything, and passed straight the fuck out. I really came over here with this drank to thank yo' lil brother for blessing me like that this morning. He rolled some big dumb-ass blunts, had me too high."

Rell plopped down in his chair. "Lil bruh got shot," he said, and reached for the bottle of Remy.

Apple gawked at Rell. "Nigga."

"Swear 'fore God," Rell said.

"Nigga," Apple repeated.

Rell nodded. "Lil niggas tried it at my daddy's building on Homan. Tried to rob us. I whooped the nigga who upped strap on us, but he got to bussin' the lil-ass gun he had. A fuckin' .25. Hit lil bruh in the stomach. On Neal, I wanna catch that nigga so bad."

Apple shook his head and took a huge bite of sandwich. He chewed and swallowed, while Rell poured himself a cup of Remy.

"I'm tellin' you what's real." Apple took a gulp of soda. "These lil niggas nowadays are a million fuckin' times worse than how we was comin' up. We used to fight. If we wanted to rob a mu'fucka, we would beat his ass and then go in his pockets. These lil niggas now act like it ain't even no such thing as fightin' no more. I don't know if it's somethin' in the water or what, but these lil fuckas don't care about shit no more. They'll kill any fuckin' body, no matter if it's a nigga they know or grew up with. It could be a blood fuckin' cousin and they'll still get down on 'em. Shit's fucked up. I keep tellin' my old lady, one of these days I'ma hit the lotto and get the fuck away from this shit for good. I'm takin' my kids and leavin'. Fuck it."

Rell smirked. "What about Dina?"

Dina was Apple's long-time girlfriend and the mother of his two sons. They all lived together across the street.

"I'm leavin' that hoe right here where I found her mu'fuckin' ass. Takin' my boys and buyin' me a crib in Jamaica some damn where."

Rell laughed. Apple laughed with him. They both knew that Apple would never leave Dina, but it sounded good. Apple and Dina had the kind of relationship that Rell wanted. They argued and fought, drank and smoked, partied and hustled and went to work, and they always came home to each other every single night. There were several girls who had crushes on Apple, just as there were guys (Rell included) who sometimes wished for just one night with Dina's sexy, thick, dark-skinned ass, but everyone knew that it was just about impossible to get either of them to cheat on the other.

"Nah, on some real shit, though," Apple said, "it's fucked up out here. If I didn't have my kids, I'd be out here in the jungle with these lil niggas. Gotta be all about family, 'cause the streets ain't playin' fair no more." He shook his head and stuffed some fries in his mouth. "Hope Jah come through a'ight."

"He'll be good. Should be walking through the door any minute now."

Rell only had about a quarter ounce of Kush left, but he didn't mind smoking it because Jah had a few pounds of the stuff. He took the sandwich bag full of Kush buds out of a front pocket, opened the bag, and put it under his nose to inhale the powerful scent. "Mmm mm mm mm mm," he said, smiling.

"Roll that shit up," Apple said.

"I will...after you break me off another piece of that sandwich."

Apple gave Rell another cold stare. He was down to the last bite of the second sandwich, and it was quite obvious that he planned on eating it himself.

"On my life, I ain't rolling up shit if you don't give me the rest of that sandwich," Rell said.

The frigid stare continued. Rell reached out and grabbed the tray. Apple didn't stop him, but it was obvious that he wanted to break Rell's hand in two as the tray slid away from him.

A man of his word, Rell slid the bag of Kush to Apple and went to work on the last of the Italian beef sandwich and fries.

Apple rolled the blunt in silence.

Just as Rell was popping the last fry in his mouth, Tamera came walking into the dining room. She sat on Rell's lap and put her head on his shoulder.

"Hey, Apple," she said sleepily, and when she only got a nod in return she turned to Rell. "Y'all ate without me?"

"Yup," Apple cut in. "Whoop his muthafuckin' ass. He bogus as hell. I told him to save you some, too. But you know how stingy that nigga is. I'd whoop his ass if I was you."

Tamera lifted her head from Rell's shoulder. A sleepy smile blossomed on her pretty brown face.

"Oh, shit. What did you do to Apple?" she said.

"I ain't did nothin', baby." Rell gave Tamera a kiss. "You know how fat people get when they eat and don't get full."

Apple raised a middle finger.

Minutes later, the three of them were sitting in a pall of heavy smoke, passing around the blunt and drinking the Remy. Somehow Tamera found a way to hook up her smartphone to the TV's surround sound in the living room, which left them listening to August Alsina until Apple complained and convinced her to switch it to Yo Gotti.

Tamera took to her own chair, scooted it over so that it was right up against Rell's, and shared the cup of Remy with him. Apple drank from his own cup. Once the first blunt was finished, Rell lit a second one.

The more Kush and Remy Rell consumed, the more he found himself thirsting for Tamera's tasty nookie. Her thighs looked so thick in the tight-fitting jeans that he leaned over in his chair and gave one of them a bite.

She giggled and slapped the back of his head. "Stop, Rell. We have company."

"So the fuck what?" He kissed her on the jaw. "I'll eat that mu'fucka in front of fat boy over there if I feel like it."

"Oh, no the hell you won't."

Rell was just about to fire back with an even nastier reply when his smartphone began ringing. Momma's contact photo came up. Shaking his head, he answered.

"I'm out here with Jah," Momma said. "Get out here and help ya brother in the house. I'ma stay upstairs in his apartment. Can't go back to my place."

"On my way out now."

Rell didn't end the call until he had the front door open and was standing on the porch. He'd expected Jah to be in a wheelchair, or being helped up the stairs by Momma and Tirzah, but Jah was walking up the stairs by himself. Tirzah and Momma were coming up behind him.

There were two police cars parked next to Ginkgo Park down on the corner of 15th and Trumbull. Rell tried not to make it so obvious that he was eyeing them as hard as he truly was. Why were they there? Had they been tipped off that Webb and Chino's killer had sped off to Trumbull Avenue? Were they watching Rell and Jah's house?

Twenty more questions ran through Rell's head, but he played it cool and focused on Jah.

"You good, bruh?" He patted Jah on the shoulder.

"Don't ask me no shit like that. You know I ain't good. A nigga done shot up the OG crib, I got a hole in my stomach — hell mu'fuckin' nah I ain't good."

Rell waited until Jah was stretched out on the living room sofa to break the news to him.

"Me and Johnny B n'em got down on the niggas who shot up the crib. It was Webb," Rell whispered to Jah. "We whacked him and that nigga Chino. That nigga Zo was there, but he got away."

"You sure it was Webb who did it?" Jah asked, peeling off his shirt to reveal the gauze bandage that was wrapped around his abdomen and lower back.

Rell nodded. "They say it was somebody in a white Benz. We saw the white Benz parked in front of Chino's house. That's what made us sit in the cut and wait to see who came out. It was Webb. Some bitch was in the Benz. Now that I think about it, I should've shot her ass, too."

Rell turned and saw that everyone was watching him and Jah. He tossed his car key to Tamera and told her to go out to the garage and get the black box out of his trunk.

Momma said, "Somebody better give me a blunt to go upstairs with. And one of y'all gotta go to the house and get my work clothes for tomorrow. I left 'em on my bed."

"I'll go and get 'em," Rell said. "In a lil while, though. Not right now. You'll have 'em sometime tonight."

"I'll be upstairs." Maria left the youngsters to themselves in Rell's apartment and headed up to Jah's place.

Tirzah stood in the dining room with her hands on her hips until Tamera came back in with the black box. Rell took it from her, set it on the coffee table next to where Jah was lying down, and snapped it open.

Inside the black box lay a fully-automatic 9 millimeter Mac-10 submachine gun and two 32-shot clips. Rell had bought the Mac-10 a year ago from a Gangster Disciple in Gary, Indiana, and had yet to use it.

Tirzah said, "Can somebody please tell me why I just got a text saying Webb got killed?"

Tamera chuckled once and shook her head. "It's a long story, sis," she said, "and hopefully it's the last chapter."

Chapter 27

"Bae, you ain't gon' believe this. Somebody done killed Webb."

"What?" The news was so shocking that PJ dropped his bar of Irish Spring soap to the shower floor.

Shalonda had just barged into the bathroom on him, which she had the right to do, since it was her bathroom he was showering in.

PJ had been staying with Shalonda for a couple of weeks now. His south side home had mysteriously caught fire earlier that month, forcing him to find somewhere else to stay, and since Shalonda had been his main squeeze at the time of the fire, he'd decided to move in with her.

He hadn't left out of the house since his uncle Stain was killed two days ago. They had gone over to a youngster named Jah's house to end the beef Jah had with Stain the way real gangsters settled their beefs — with bullets. Unfortunately, things had not gone as planned.

PJ had been sitting in the driver's seat, waiting on Stain and Jamie, one of Stain's partners, to get out of the back seat of a car he'd rented from a dope fiend for a few bags of heroin. Stain had toted an AK-47, and Jamie had been strapped with a 12-gauge shotgun.

But just as Stain and Jamie were emerging from the rear doors, the back door of the house on 13th and Avers had swung open and a young nigga who looked a lot like a light-skinned version of Jah had come running out blasting at them. Then a female had come from the side of the house blasting another gun at PJ, Stain, and Jamie.

PJ sped off quick enough to save himself from any harm, but not quick enough to save his uncle. When he looked to the back seat, he'd seen Uncle Stain hanging halfway out of the open rear passenger door with a bunch of bullet wounds in his chest and one in the side of his head. PJ had abandoned the car at the spot where he'd left his chameleon-painted Chevy Tahoe and raced off to Shalonda's house on 16th Street and St. Louis Avenue, and he hadn't left since. Shalonda had gotten him enough weed to last him through the days, and he had a kilo and a half of heroin and close to $200,000 in drug money in a suitcase in her bedroom, so he could afford to sit in the house without working for a while.

The only reason he was upset about Webb being dead was because Webb owed him $9,500. No matter how much money PJ managed to accumulate, no amount was ever too petty for him to collect. He'd lived so long without a dime that now he cherished every penny.

"Yeah," Shalonda went on, "he got hit up on Homan. Him and this nigga named Chino. Damn, man, I used to hang out with Chino all the time. That is so sad. I feel bad for his kids. He got two boys and a girl by Tanasia."

"That nigga Webb owed me ten racks. Shit."

"I know. That's why I told you. I just found out. My sister Tangie just texted me saying she walked past with Momma right after it happened. She say this young nigga named Zo might've had somethin' to do with it, said she saw him walkin' off the other way lookin' suspicious. I don't know what's goin' on. Let me do some more fishin'. I'll let you know what's up when you get out the shower."

Shalonda left him alone in the bathroom, and he washed and rinsed hurriedly. For some reason, he wanted to hurry up and get to the .45-caliber Ruger he had laying on top of his clothes on the toilet seat. There were way too many bodies dropping in this one neighborhood for him not to have his gun in reach at all times.

PJ was a huge, dark man. A lot of people he'd met on the south side called him Rozay, because he looked a lot like the rapper Rick Ross — a fat, black street nigga with a thick beard and an endless artwork of tattoos all over his chest, arms, belly, and back.

He stepped out of the shower and dried off while holding his pistol. He lifted the curtain that hung over the bathroom window and glanced out to the alley where his SUV was parked. It sat close to the wrought iron fence just outside Shalonda's backyard, its chrome 28-inch rims shining in the reflection of the light pole that towered over it.

PJ put on a pair of boxer-briefs and socks and then sat down on the toilet seat to step into his blue jeans.

"The fuck is goin' on around here?" he mumbled, shaking his head. "Niggas gettin' killed left and right. A muthafucka done killed my uncle. Block so hot a nigga can't even go out and make no money." Another shake of the head. "I need to take my ass back to Georgia."

Shalonda and her two daughters, Ebony and Nae Nae, were sitting at the kitchen table eating dinner when PJ came out of the bathroom. He put the gun on his hip and sat down, staring at Shalonda, whose eyes were on her smartphone while she forked macaroni and cheese into her mouth. PJ had already devoured two plates, and if not for the children, he knew he'd be on his third.

"Oh yeah, it's official," Shalonda said. "It's right here on ABC7 News. 'North Lawndale murders escalate; two men killed on the 1500 block of Homan Avenue, bringing the total number of killings in this neighborhood up to ten for this month and leaving many in the community in fear'. See, PJ, you're doing right by keeping your ass in the house. Let these goofies kill each other all they want. I heard our weed man just got shot too. It ain't safe out there for nobody."

"Hold on, you said our weed man got hit up?"

Shalonda nodded her head yes, not once bothering to look up from her phone. "Yup. Jah got shot over on Homan, in his daddy's building."

If Shalonda had not been so glued to her smartphone, she would have seen the shock on PJ's face. He hadn't told her that it was Jah he'd been after when his uncle was killed, so he couldn't blame her for not telling him that the guy she'd bought the Kush from was Jah. Now, though, he wished he had told her.

"Jah?" he said. "Which Jah? I know a few of 'em."

"Jah off 13th and Avers. Rell's lil brother." Finally, she raised her eyes from the phone screen and looked at PJ. "You know what? Come to think of it, when Jah brought us that loud, he asked me about your truck. He stared at it for a minute, then asked me about it. It kinda threw me off a little. I meant to tell you that."

PJ just stared at her. He couldn't believe that she'd let something so critical go without warning him. It took him a long moment to think of what to say next.

"So," PJ asked, "it was Jah who sold us the Kush, huh? The orange-lookin' shit."

"Mm hmm."

"A'ight. I need some more of that shit. Call him right now and see what's up."

Chapter 28

The bullet had spiraled right through Jah's left side and exited his back. The only real damage was to his ribcage, and according to the doctor, it would heal and be like new within the next 30-45 days.

Lying on the sofa with his feet propped up on Tirzah's lap, listening as Tamera filled her in on what had happened to Webb, Jah was feeling more anger than pain. Sure, Webb was dead, but the three main people Jah really wanted dead — E, Zo, and Chris — were still alive and well.

He logged into his Facebook account and found eighteen new inbox messages and a bunch of notifications. People were posting worried messages on his page. The inbox messages were all from his friends. They wanted to know what the fuck had happened and where they could find the guy who'd shot him.

He made one post:

"I'm good yall it wuz juss a stomach shot yall know how im rockin bout it on neal"

He didn't stick around to see the comments. Instead, he logged out and went to his text messages. He had three of them: two from Felicia and one from Shalonda. The first message from Felicia, sent around the time he'd been shot, was about Dora needing more diapers. The second, sent when he'd been in the hospital, was a prayer for good health and recovery.

The text message from Shalonda was a request for an ounce of Kush.

He replied to Felicia and told her that she could stop by and pick up the money for the diapers. He had almost $2,100 in cash in his pocket, and he never hesitated to provide for his daughter.

He typed a message to Shalonda letting her know that he'd just left the hospital with a bullet wound to the stomach, but that he would get the ounce of Kush to her within the next few hours.

"What you doing over there, nigga?" Rell asked from the dining room.

"Shit," Jah said. "Fuckin' around on the book. Everybody gettin' at me actin' worried and shit. They need to be worried about the lil niggas that pulled it."

Tirzah rubbed his leg. "I bet you Zo and them other dudes are already out of town. Everybody knows how you are when it comes to beef. They gotta be scared as shit. I know I would be."

"It's all good." Jah picked up the Mac-10 from the coffee table and loaded in a magazine.

"Be careful, bruh," Rell warned. "That's a fully. You'll be done emptied the whole clip on accident."

"I got this." Jah put the gun back in the flat little black box and studied Tirzah's pretty face as she used her tongue to seal a blunt of Kush.

He thought of Rell and Johnny B getting down on Webb and Chino and wished he'd have been there to get his own hands dirty. Usually it was him who took care of all the drama. Rell had gotten out of the game a while ago, after his prison bid, but here lately, no thanks to Jah, he was being pulled right back in.

Jah looked at his big brother and slowly shook his head.

"What?" Rell said, passing a blunt to Apple.

"I just feel bad, bruh," Jah said. "I pulled you into all this shit when D-Lo got whacked and it's been nonstop drama ever since. It's all my mu'fuckin' fault."

Rell shook his head. "No, it ain't. I'm a grown-ass man, lil bruh. You better believe that I am more than capable of avoiding whatever I wanna avoid. If I get in some shit, it's because that's what I wanted to do. It ain't nobody's fault but mine."

Jah nodded his head, but deep down, his feelings remained the same. He felt that he was dragging big bro back into this shit, and it was not a good feeling.

Kush smoke filled the air. For the next few minutes, they listened to Yo Gotti and smoked. Jah gazed at Tirzah and couldn't stop smiling. Thanks to Rell and Tamera's attraction to each other, he had scored big with Tirzah, who just so happened to be the baddest girl he'd ever had.

He lay there smoking blunts with her until his eyes became too heavy to hold open. Then he slept.

King Rio

Chapter 29

"So, what's your net worth? Or is that too much to ask?"

"No, it's fine. $12.8 million. Not bad for a nerdy white kid from Connecticut, huh?"

Yes! Susan thought to herself as she lay face down on the soft leather massage table. She almost jumped up and did a dance. A money dance.

Chuck Calloway was on the table directly beside hers. His masseuse was a slender Asian girl, and hers was a young Black woman.

"Wow," Susan said. "I've never met a millionaire. I mean, I've probably crossed paths with some, but I don't know of any personally."

"It's not as fun as you'd think it would be. Just a bunch of family and friends who all of a sudden love you to death. People asking you to buy them cars and homes. I swear, I've heard some of the craziest excuses. Some of them are just too outrageous. Like my cousin Ed, who broke his arm during a camping trip — you don't wanna know how — and asked me for two hundred fucking grand to get it fixed. Said he didn't have health insurance. Then when I bought him a Mustang he wanted me to buy him a Ferrari to go with it. Oh, and then there's my mom's brother, who's still mad at me to this day for not giving him a million bucks to build a restaurant in New Jersey. What an asshole he is. I just try to save as much as possible. I look out for my mom when she needs things. She got $700,000 and two houses when Dad passed but that doesn't mean I can't help out, you know what I mean? It's the least I can do. I've got about $4 million in the bank, and another $8.5 million in properties. My cars are worth about a quarter mill. And I've got some jewelry."

"You're doing right, Chuck. Take care of your mother. God will bless you for doing it. But screw those family members. I have some of them myself, and I refuse to give them a single dime of my money. I'm not even going to leave anything to them when I go. My life insurance policies leave everything to my husband, and if he's not alive to get it, all of it will go to his boys. As much as I don't like the little fuckers, I think they need it most, and they'd be a lot more grateful for it than my blood relatives."

"You're really something." Chuck laughed. "I understand, though. Money is the root of all evil."

"It truly is."

Susan's smartphone began ringing, and she knew that it was Big Man. No one else ever called her.

The phone was in her purse, which was on the floor next to the massage table.

"Is that your phone?" Chuck asked.

"Yeah. I'll ignore it. I know who it is."

"The guy from Soyka?"

"The worst mistake of my life," Susan corrected.

She wasn't being completely honest. The truth was, Susan loved her husband dearly - always had since their first date. She knew that she was only trying to convince herself to go along with whatever this was because her life had become boring and depressing and she wanted something new.

"Let me tell you about my living arrangement," she said to Chuck, "and I want your honest to God opinion."

"Go for it," Chuck said.

"Well...are you familiar with Chicago? The ghettos of Chicago, I mean. The areas of the city that are better known as Chiraq, where all the gangbanging and shootings go on."

"I've read about it. Spike Lee's doing a film about it. Saw that in the Miami Herald a few months back."

"Would you ever live there?"

Chuck took a couple of seconds to reply. "Hell no, I wouldn't." He scoffed. "There's no way in hell I'd live in that kind of environment. I've never been shot before, but I assume it's not a good feeling."

"Yeah, well, I live in one of those areas, and my husband is too cheap to move us somewhere safe."

"I can compromise on a lot of things, but my safety's not one of them."

112

"Exactly. That's why I don't want to be married anymore. That's why I'd rather just stay here in Miami. My husband's children are gang members. One of them was just shot today. The other only recently was released from prison. They smoke weed and carry guns. I mean, these guys are literally real-life gang members, and my husband wants to keep them around. He wants to stay there in Chicago for them. I don't want to put up with that."

"Can't say that I blame you for that, to be honest. I'm with you. In fact, I don't think you can find a single person in this entire hotel who wouldn't be with you on that. He's a jerk for even suggesting you stay there. You're more than welcome to bring your stuff to my condo and stay with me until you find a place. Or I could set you up in one of my houses."

"I'd love that."

"Which do you mean?"

"Whichever is best for you. I've got my own money. Not as much as you, but I've got a nice amount saved up."

"How soon are you trying to make the move? We could do it first thing tomorrow. I have a conference call and a few meetings in the morning but aside from that my schedule's pretty clear."

Just then, Chuck and Susan's long massage came to an end. They sat up on the tables, stared at each other, and then stood.

Standing there before Chuck, gazing up at his cute face, Susan decided to go for it. She got up on her tippy toes and pressed her lips to his. His hands went to her back, and he returned the kiss. He knew what he was doing, too. He was a much better kisser than Big Man, who hardly ever kissed her at all.

"Let's just see where this goes between us tonight," Susan said, beaming as she picked up her purse and slipped her robe back on. "Where to now?"

"The room?" Chuck suggested.

"Sounds like a plan to me."

Chapter 30

"Woo, this that shit they didn't want me on
    I'm 'bout to act a badonkadonk, shamone, shamone
    Don't need sugar, I need cream, I'm dark and strong
    The garbage man puttin' on cologne, aroma wrong
    I'm on, I'm on, this that shit they didn't want
    I act a ass and shit a skunk, I will, I won't
    Black your eye like will.i.am, you Willy Wonka
    That's me in the Lam, I'm disappearin' like Jimmy Hoffa
    AK-47 my business partner, business is well
    French kiss a bitch, she don't speak French, can't kiss and tell
    I push his ass in the wishin' well, then wish him well
    Sippin' syrup like ginger ale, but I'm the quickest snail
    From here to Hell, I hear them hail, I give them hell
    I'm spittin' hail, I'm Clinton, well, I did inhale
    These niggas frail, they Chip and Dale, they little girls
    Watch me act a donkey, then pin a tail, spit out your nails
    Uh, glory, hallelujah
    Holy shit, I'm the holy shit, I'm God's manure
    I know how to hack a jeweller ward and not computers
    I meditate like a Buddhist, Holy ramen noodles
    And now you sleep, I'm inside your room wit' a lot of shooters
    You wake up to this chopper tool, it's like, 'Cock-a-doodle'
    I'm awkward, cuckoo, I turn your Froot Loop to chocolate Yoo-
Hoo
    I'm hotter than Honolulu, glory unto you, glory..."

    Zo saw the stunned look on Tangela's face when he pulled up to the curb on 15th and Christiana in the clean white 1989 Chevrolet Caprice, bumping Lil Wayne's "Glory". He sat there for a minute, lighting a Newport and scrolling down his Facebook page on the smartphone he'd gotten earlier.
    The car had been parked in an empty lot next to its owner's home on 16th and Central Park with a big "For Sale" sign in its back

window for a few months now. It had white 26-inch rims, custom red leather interior, and five 12-inch speakers in the trunk. Although Zo had told a bunch of people that the car would one day be his, he'd never believed it. But for the low price of $6,500 and one of the ounces of heroin he'd gotten out of Webb's Gucci backpack (Renny, a dope fiend from around the way, had confirmed that the substance was indeed heroin), Zo had been able to purchase the box Chevy and ride off into the sunset.

Tangie and two other girls were standing on the front porch of a house in the middle of the block with their hands in their coat pockets and their eyes on the Chevy.

Zo was not only riding clean, he was also riding dirty with the Tec-9 on his lap. Webb's backpack occupied the passenger seat. Zo had initially considered going to pick up E and Chris, but he was too embarrassed by Chris's swollen and battered face to have him in the new whip and he knew that E was with Chris, so he said fuck both of them and didn't even phone them with the news of his Chevy come-up. They'd find out eventually, anyway, and he wanted at least one night with the car all to himself.

Well, maybe not exactly to himself.

He wouldn't mind having Tangie's sexy red-boned ass sitting next to him tonight. She was his biggest crush - always had been since grade school. She was one of those reddish-brown skinned girls with hair down to her ass and a flawless body with just enough curves to make the guys stare every time they saw her.

Tangie walked down the stairs and knocked on his passenger window. He turned to her and grinned, as if he was just now seeing her. He lowered the music volume and the window.

"Ummm," Tangie said, sucking her teeth, "niggas are tryna sleep around here. People got work tomorrow. It's nine o'clock. You can take this hot-ass stolen car down the street somewhere. Please and thank you."

"Stolen? This car ain't stolen. I bought this." Zo's grin grew wider.

"With what, a gun?"

"Nope." Zo unzipped the backpack and stretched it open to show her all the cash it held. "Bought it with this."

Her expression changed instantly. She went from looking at him with disgust to practically drooling over the loot.

"Get in," he said, taking full advantage of the situation.

Tangie turned to her friends and shouted that she'd be right back. Zo zipped up the backpack and tossed it over to the backseat as Tangie pulled open the passenger door and got in.

Her eyes examined every inch of the Chevy's interior as Zo drove off and made a right onto 15th. She had on a thick red jacket over jeans and Jordans. Her hair was straightened and dyed blonde. Hanging from the thin gold necklace on her neck was a pendant that spelled out her name in gold letters.

"Do you have a license?" she asked. "And you need to move that gun. Put it up under the seat or something."

"Hell nah. Why would I do that? You heard what happened to Webb and Chino earlier? Shit is serious out here right now."

She turned her back to her door and crossed her arms, staring at him. "Of course I heard what happened. Me and my momma walked right past you on 16th before we got to Homan, and we saw Webb laid out in the front yard at Chino's house."

"Don't say it like that, like I had somethin' to do with that shit. I heard them yoppas goin' off and took flight."

"Yeah, whatever. How'd you get all this money? And that outfit? Come on now, Zo. I wasn't born yesterday. You did something to somebody."

Shaking his head, Zo raised his right hand. "Honest to God truth, I didn't rob no nigga for this bread." He paused, juggling whether or not to tell her the full story. He figured telling her a little of it wouldn't hurt. "A'ight. I'll admit I was there. But on my grandma, all I did was pick up the bag. Some niggas came out the cut wit' choppas just as we was walkin' out the door. Webb had just took me shoppin'."

"Why would he take you shopping? Come on, Zo. Really?"

"On my grandma, I ain't lyin'," Zo swore. He saw the excitement in her eyes. She was only questioning him to keep herself in the clear. Once she made sense of it all he knew she'd be down to ride with him. "You still don't believe me? We can go and ask my sister right now. She was right there on the porch with me when Webb came and picked me up."

"Why'd he come and pick you up?"

A-ha. There it was. The key to Zo's entire involvement with Webb lay there.

When Zo had been in his sister's kitchen with E and Chris, listening to the King Louie music his little brother was playing and thinking of a way to get at Jah first, he'd thought back to what Leon had just told him about the other guys Jah was beefing with — the CVLs off Millard, and Webb.

Luckilyy for Zo, one of his sister's friends was one of the many neighborhood girls Webb was fucking, and she'd been able to get Webb's phone number from the girl.

The rest was history.

Zo had called Webb and expressed that he was interested in doing something to Jah, because Jah had beat up one of his friends. Webb pulled up thirty minutes later with the girl in the white Benz to pick him up.

"He came and got me 'cause I owed him some money," Zo lied as he made a right turn onto Kedzie.

"You's a goddamn lie, Zo. You ain't never in your life had no money."

"How you gon' tell me what the fuck I had? Damn, I'm telling you the truth. A'ight? You can take that shit or leave that shit but that's what it is."

Tangie sucked her teeth, uncrossed her arms, and shifted her eyes to the road ahead. She looked incredibly sexy doing it. Zo noticed then that her lipstick matched her jacket, and that she smelled like she'd been smoking weed.

"How much money is in that bag?" she asked.

"Enough."

"Asshole."

Zo laughed. "Why, what you wanna do?"

"Get some weed. It's a shame you into it with Jah n'em 'cause my sister say he got the best loud out here right now. Some orange Kush. I want some of that shit so fuckin' bad."

"We can have yo' sister buy it for us, can't we?"

"I don't know. Probably. Let's stop by her house right quick. You remember where she stay, right? On St. Louis?"

"How could I forget?" Zo said, and pressed down a little more on the gas pedal. "You know how much I love Shalonda."

King Rio

Chapter 31

Rell had started off by sitting Tamera on the dresser and sucking on her clitoris until she convulsed in orgasm, and now it felt like his dick was splitting her in two.

Tamera's mouth was agape and her body was bouncing on the bed as Rell held her knees up to her ears and punished her with deep, rough strokes.

She couldn't stop herself from moaning. They were loud moans. Ridiculously loud. But then again, Rell's dick was also ridiculously big, so it balanced out.

Tirzah pounded at the bedroom door.

"Tamera! Bitch, it is not that serious!"

If only you knew, Tamera thought as Rell's relentless thrusts continued.

The Remy Martin they had consumed with Apple had Tamera feeling good and freaky. She was loving every bit of the rough sex she was receiving, though it hurt every time he sank all the way in. She could take the length of him with no problem; it was the girth of him that hurt. His dick was too fat. It stretched her wide and deep, resulting in a feeling that was both blissful and painful.

The only items of clothing the two of them had on were socks. Everything else was scattered across the floor beside the bed. Someone (Tirzah, more than likely) had turned up the heat to a temperature so high that their skin was slippery with sweat.

Just ten minutes into this particular episode, Tamera tensed up and shivered as an orgasm sent her fingernails deep into Rell's back. He pushed all the way in and stayed there, kissing at her lips and neck.

"Damn, this shit good," he whispered in her ear. "You okay?"

She could not respond. The orgasm was too overwhelming. Her vaginal muscles were still contracting around his huge phallus. This was the best sex she'd ever had.

Staring up at Rell, taking in the sight of his perfect face and bulging muscles and rich brown skin, and the tattoos that covered his broad chest, Tamera knew that no dream could compete with the reality of this moment. She was looking at the finest man she'd ever laid eyes on. Never in a million years could she have imagined herself with a Black man as fine as Rell, and she could tell by the hungry look in his eyes that he was feeling the same way about her.

"Let me know when you're good," he said. "I ain't done with your lil sexy ass. Not yet."

"You're killing me, Rell." She had tears in her eyes.

"That's my intention."

"No, I'm serious. I'm, like, about to die. Your dick is not human." She laughed, and he laughed with her.

He pulled out and moved back on his knees, lowering his face to kiss the insides of her thighs before signaling for her to turn over.

"You already know how I want it." He wore the cheesiest of smiles. He was breathing hard and obviously ready to give her a lot more.

Slowly, she turned over on all fours and then buried her face in a pillow. She felt his hands slide all across her ass before they latched onto her waist. She felt the head of his dick on her pussy, and she hoped that he would take it easy, for a few seconds, at least.

She had no such luck.

He slam-dunked into her. She gasped and bit the pillow.

"Aw, yeah. This is it right here. Stay just like this. Don't move." He put a hand on the middle of her back as he fucked her. "You like it like this? Tell me. Let me know how much you like it."

She turned her head so that her mouth wasn't in the pillow. "Yes. Yes. I love...uhh, mmm, uhh, ohh...I love it!"

"Throw this mu'fucka back then."

Tamera found the energy to follow his orders. Looking over her shoulder at him, she threw her ass back so hard that it made loud slapping sounds against him. He leaned back a little, thoroughly enjoying every second of it. She had no idea how her poor little nookie was taking his huge pole so effortlessly. It was a miracle that she had not yet died from the pounding he was giving her.

Just then, Tirzah came to the door again.

"Will y'all please hurry up in there? Jah wants me to go and drop off this weed and I don't wanna go by myself."

"Just go, nigga!" Rell said over Tamera's incessant moans. He pushed all the way in and held it there. "Damn, you need a babysitter to go with you?"

"Umm, I believe I was talking to my sister. Last time I checked, her name was Tamera."

Rell went back to hammering Tirzah's sister. Slap slap slap slap slap. Her ass bounced and jiggled. She moaned like a pornstar, and Rell heard Tirzah's footfalls as she stomped off down the hallway.

He grinned proudly.

Ten more minutes of sliding his dick in and out of Tamera's snug nookie is what it took to bring him to the edge.

He pulled out and sprayed her back and ample derrière with half a dozen ribbons of semen.

Chapter 32

"I just got a text from Jah. He's sending the Kush with his girl," Shalonda said as she sat Indian-style on the sofa.

Tangie, her younger sister, was sitting next to her, and the young nigga who'd brought Tangie here was sitting at the opposite end of the other sofa where PJ sat with his gun on his lap.

PJ nodded his head, but kept quiet. He didn't want to reveal his position. Mentally, though, his mind was running wild with new plans. He had not considered that Jah might send someone else with the Kush. This threw a wrench in PJ's plans. He'd wanted to just walk outside and shoot Jah dead to avenge the murder of his uncle, then flee to his hometown in Georgia. His family would be proud of him for doing it. Though hardly anyone in the family had actually liked Stain, now everyone was distraught over his death. Many members of the family were already getting ready to fly and drive to Chicago for Stain's funeral.

PJ wanted Jah dead before Stain's burial.

"I heard about you. PJ, right?" It was the boy who'd brought Tangie over.

PJ looked over at him. "How the fuck you hear about me?"

"My sister's boyfriend say you got some money on Jah's head. Plus, I was with Webb earlier. He spoke on you. Said he needed to talk to you or some shit."

"Yeah, that nigga Webb owed me fifteen bands," PJ said, exaggerating the sum of money Webb had owed him. He studied the boy's fresh appearance. "What's your name again?"

"Zo." He stretched across the empty space between him PJ and shook the fat guy's hand. "I'm one of the Travs off Spaulding. I'm a young nigga, but I'm known out in these streets."

Tangie sucked her teeth and gave Zo a brief stare - brief because she and Shalonda were busy being nosy on Shalonda's Facebook page.

Zo chuckled. "She hatin' 'cause I just bought that Chevy. Hate that a nigga so young out here flexin' on these lames."

"You know what happened to Webb?" PJ asked.

Zo nodded but said nothing.

"You seen it?"

Zo looked across the room at Tangie and Shalonda, then turned back to PJ. "Yeah. I didn't see their faces, but when I looked outside, I saw one of the cars. It was Jah's brother's car. Tamera from the building on Homan was in the driver's seat."

PJ clenched his teeth together and knitted his brows. As badly as he wanted to hide his true intentions, it came tumbling out of his mouth.

"I'm killin' that punk-ass nigga! They killed my uncle. I can't wait to catch up with them niggas."

Shalonda and Tangie gasped in unison.

"Join the crowd," Zo said, digging a Tec-9 out of his Gucci bag. "I'm emptyin' this mu'fucka at dude n'em on sight. On Neal. Shit, Jah gon' try to get me, anyway. Might as well get him first. We tried to rob him and his brother earlier and he ended up gettin' shot. I know Jah. He gon' try to whack me and my niggas soon's he see us, and I ain't goin' out like that."

PJ nodded thoughtfully. He could already tell that he was going to like Zo, if only for the fact that they shared an enemy.

"It's all good," he said. "Ain't no talkin'. We gon' let these guns talk."

Shalonda said, "Wait a minute. So, y'all got beef with Jah and Rell? What in the world have I gotten myself into? PJ, you could've told me that Jah was the one y'all was into it with! What the fuck, man! And now his girl is on the way over here. Don't do nothing to that girl. Just buy the weed and let her go on about her business. She ain't did shit to nobody."

"Man, fuck that bitch," Zo said quickly. "She can get it, too. Fuck you talm'bout." What he meant was "What the fuck are you talking about?" but it came out differently.

Still clenching his teeth, PJ thought of the girl Jah was sending over and tried to think of what he would do to her when she arrived.

Shooting her was out of the question. Kidnapping didn't make much sense either since he knew that Jah didn't have much money.

PJ came to the conclusion that a good beat-down was the answer. And maybe he could use her to get Jah and his brother right where he wanted them. Then he could get some payback before Uncle Stain's dead body was even in the ground.

Chapter 33

Janky was the nickname of Tamera's cherry-red Ford Taurus, and for good reason. The rear driver's side door didn't open. The rear passenger's side door's window didn't roll down. The heat worked when it felt like working, which wasn't often. Only one windshield wiper worked. The gas was permanently stuck on E, so one could never tell if the tank was empty or not. And now both the driver's window and the one behind it had black plastic bags taped over them because they had been punched out by the angry father of a girl Tirzah beat up a few days ago.

"In there letting that nigga knock your uterus outta place," Tirzah complained as she adjusted the seat and rearview mirror to her liking. "You need to be getting him to put your name on the deed to this house. Or at least get you a new car. Something better than this piece of shit."

She turned the key in the ignition and got mad when the engine stalled. "Come on, Janky. Work with me. I didn't mean to call you a piece of shit, okay? Work with Momma." She tried again and got the same result. "You dirty bitch, you better fuckin' start!" She punched the steering wheel (the horn was also broken) and turned the key once again.

This time it was a success. The engine rumbled to life, bringing a warm smile to Tirzah's cold face.

"That's what I'm talking about, baby. I see you need some tough love today. Don't worry, I'll beat you like Ike beat Tina if you don't get me to 16th and St. Louis and back."

She tried turning on the heat and found that her luck had run dry. There was only a clicking sound and then nothing.

"Son of a bitch." Tirzah put it in drive and maneuvered Janky out of the parking space between Rell's car and Maria's SUV.

She rubbed her hands together and blew some hot air between them as she made it to the corner of 15th and Trumbull. "I'm way too fucking high to be putting up with this cold-ass weather," she muttered vacantly.

But it would be worth it. $400 for an ounce of Kush, and Jah was going to let her keep $100 for herself. Not bad for a five-minute trip. Shalonda lived right around the corner with the fat guy who'd moved from the south side because his house had burned down.

Tirzah took 15th to Homan and then Homan to 16th, already spending the money in her head. She would get the Paul Mitchell hairdryer she'd been wanting to get for months now. Since she made most of her money doing hair, it would be a wise investment. The hairdryer she had at hers and Tamera's apartment was old and nearly as raggedy as Janky.

It wasn't until Tirzah made it to the corner of 16th and St. Louis that she realized where she was going, and when she did, she gasped in disbelief and immediately stomped on the brake pedal.

Shalonda's boyfriend was PJ.

PJ was Stain's nephew.

Just a few days ago, after learning about the beef that Jah had with Stain, Tirzah had suggested that Jah and Rell rob PJ. She'd told them that PJ had long money, and that he was staying with a girl on St. Louis Avenue, but she hadn't told them the girl's name, and the conversation had never come up again.

"What the fuck am I doing?" She was right in front of Shalonda's house, and there was a fat man in a green leather Pelle Pelle jacket walking down the porch stairs.

It was PJ. All three hundred-something pounds of him.

Tirzah was struck by the burgeoning inclination to speed away, just in case PJ had figured out what she had just figured out. But judging from the way he was moving, casually glancing around the block, not in much of a hurry to get to her, she decided to go ahead with the deal.

The street was dark; lately, the youngsters had taken to shooting out the street lights in an effort to keep both the police and their enemies from spotting them outside at night.

PJ was mere feet from the passenger door when the plastic on Tirzah's window was suddenly torn open.

Frightened, she turned to her window and found herself staring down the barrel of a submachine gun.

It took her half a second to realize that Zo was the gunman.

"Get the fuck out the car, bitch," he hissed. "Don't make me say it twice."

Chapter 34

Susan awoke feeling groggy, so incredibly fatigued that her legs gave out and she went crashing to the floor next to the bed.

The room spun like a windmill. She saw three doors with three identical high-heeled shoes laying beside them, three beds with identical sheets and blankets. The door became one door, then two, then three again.

She shut her eyes, hoping that the spell of dizziness would pass.

"David," she murmured four seconds before she remembered that she had not been with her husband before she went to bed.

Wait...had she gone to bed? She didn't remember ever going to bed. Chuck. That was his name. She'd come back to the room with Chuck, and they'd had another drink. She had started kissing him on the sofa. He had sucked on her breasts and told her how much he wanted to be with her.

Then things got blurry.

She remembered being in a shower, with water splashing down on her face, but that was it. Nothing else came to mind.

"David." She called on her husband again, knowing that he wasn't here but still longing for his presence.

Then she called for Chuck.

He didn't answer, either.

Twenty minutes or so of opening and closing her eyes was what it took to finally make the three doors turn into one.

She noticed that she was naked. Her bracelet was gone. Her purse was nowhere to be found. She could not even locate her smartphone.

She could not stand, so she crawled all around the room and finally out the door. She found the phone and tried to dial Big Man's phone number. She dialed the wrong number five times before she finally reached him.

"Dave..."

"Jesus Christ, Susan. Where are you? I've been calling you for the last four damn hours. I had to get another car. Why'd you take the car without letting me know about it? Where are you?"

Susan had to think. "The Grove Isle Hotel," she said finally.

"What are you doing there?"

"Just come and get me!" She slammed down the phone, collapsed onto her back on the soft beige carpet, and stared up at the ceiling.

"Big Man's gonna kill me," she muttered to herself.

She took in a deep, settling breath. A few minutes passed, and she was finally able to stand up with the aid of a hand on the wall.

She went back to the bedroom and found her dress and heels, but everything else — her purse, necklace, tennis bracelet, and earrings — was gone.

"That fucker." She struggled into her dress and five-inch heels. The reality of what had happened to her was just setting in.

Chuck Calloway — if that was even his real name — had drugged her and then robbed her of all her things.

She fell across the sofa and lay there, thinking of how she was going to explain this to David. She couldn't tell him that she'd been here to see another man, so it would have to be a woman. But what reason did she have to come here with a woman?

A spa treatment. She'd met...no, she had a friend who lived here in Miami. Linda was an old friend, from high school. She'd come here for a spa treatment with Linda, who'd turned out to be a woman who was now terribly addicted to drugs. Linda had stolen all of her things when she fell asleep after a few drinks.

There. Simple as that. She would give the fictional story to Big Man and stick with it, whether he believed it or not.

Once she'd gathered up enough strength to leave the room, she went out and got on the elevator. She slid down on the cool steel wall as it began its descent to the lobby, and she didn't stand again until the door opened.

"Ma'am...are you alright?"

It was a man's voice. He stood just outside of the elevator, perhaps waiting to get on. She hardly noticed him as she walked out into the lobby, but he was at her side until she found a seat in a chair near the receptionist desk.

She looked at him.

He was big and as pale as a corpse, with bushy eyebrows and an aquiline nose. His tie was dull brown, shirt white, glasses tortoise shell, slacks gray. He looked like a cop, in Susan's opinion.

"You, uhh...been drinking? You don't look too well," he said, hunched over her. "I'm Detective Johnson, Miami PD."

"I'm fine." Susan dropped her head back and sighed. The lights were bright in the lobby. They shined through her eyelids.

"You sure, ma'am? Because you sure don't look fine."

"I said I'm fine. My husband's on his way here to get me now. I'll be perfectly fine." She sat forward, squinting against the light as she peeked at the man's face.

He was in the chair beside hers, watching her closely. For a moment there were two of him.

"I'm here because we received a tip that one of our most wanted fugitives was spotted here at this hotel, with a woman who fits your description." He put a hand on her knee and gave it a reassuring squeeze. "The guy's name is Johnathan Bellingham. He's a notorious rapist out of Orange County in California, recently paroled from prison. Two days ago he drugged and raped a woman in the bathroom at Soyka. It's a restaurant not far from here. We're really, really looking for this guy. Tall, handsome, White male — any chance you might've crossed paths with him?"

"I have no clue who or what you're talking about," Susan said. "I've been drinking a little, that's all. I'm here alone. I'm fine."

Just then, the sound of Big Man's huge voice boomed across the lobby:

"Susan!"

It took every ounce of energy in her to stand up and walk to him without collapsing to the floor. When she made it to him she fell into his arms.

"Jesus, Susan. You okay? I've been worried sick."

"Yeah, I...it was Linda. An old friend of mine. She got me drunk and stole all my stuff, the dirty bitch. She's strung out on heroin. I had no idea."

"Come on. Let's get you to the car." He wrapped an arm around her shoulder and walked her outside.

There was a white Ford sedan parked just outside the hotel's front entrance. He led her to it and helped her into the passenger seat.

"Where's the Bentley?" Big Man asked as he secured her seatbelt.

"Valet."

"I'll send for it in the morning. First I've gotta get you to bed."

"I'm not that drunk, Dave. I'm okay. Sheesh." Susan looked him dead in the eyes and tried not to look as dizzy as she felt. The sky was pitch-black, and she wondered what time it was. She waited for Big Man to get in the driver's seat and then added, "I'm hungry. I want a burger."

"You look like hell."

"I look like I need a burger."

The time on the car radio read 11:22 P.M.

Susan looked out her window and saw the police detective standing there with his hands on his waistline as Big Man drove off. A part of her wanted to tell the detective that yes, she had probably been drugged and raped by Johnathan Bellingham, but she thought it would only put her in hot water with Big Man, and she already felt horrible for attempting to cheat on him with the rapist in the first place.

"Where'd you like to go for that burger?" Big Man asked.

Susan sighed and stared straight ahead. The dizziness was slowly leaving her, but it was still there. It felt like her brain was doing a tornado-spin in her skull. Her fingers were trembling. Her heart was beating at an abnormal pace.

"You look like shit, Susan," Big Man said.

"Yeah, well, you smell like shit quite often," she fired back, "but I don't give you hell about it."

He chuckled once. "There's my wife. Thought I'd lost you for a minute there."

Chapter 35

It was taking Tirzah far too long to return from the drug run.

After twenty minutes, Jah sat up on the sofa and dialed her mobile number, feeling woozy and tired from the Vicodin he'd been given for his wound, but not too sluggish to realize that Tirzah should have been back by now. His brows came together when the call went to voicemail.

He gazed emptily at the Mac-10 on the table for a brief moment. Apple had just left in Rell's car to get food for everyone, and it sounded like Rell and Tamera were on their third try at making a baby in the bedroom.

Jah stood up. It didn't hurt as much as he thought it would. He picked up the Mac-10 and went to the living room window. He used the barrel to separate the ugly maroon curtain.

Tamera's car wasn't parked out front.

He returned to the sofa and decided to wait a while longer. Tirzah had probably delivered the Kush to Shalonda and then went somewhere to spend the $100 she'd made off the deal. Probably went in a store somewhere and left her phone in the car.

His mind went to the robbery that had ended with him being shot, and again he wished he'd been around when Rell had seen Zo at Chino's house. Zo would certainly be just as dead as Webb and Chino.

"Can't believe them lil muthafuckas tried to stick us up," he said to himself as he grabbed the TV remote control off the coffee table and turned to the news.

He was just turning up the volume on an abc7 News story about Webb and Chino's shooting deaths when someone knocked at the door.

"It's me, y'all," Maria said.

Jah sighed and shook his head, wishing that someone else could open the front for him. He got up and went to the door. As soon as he got it open, Momma started tripping.

"I know damn well somebody else could've answered this goddamn door. The hell is going on in here? Rell! Get'cho lazy ass out here right goddamn now. And I mean it."

Jah laughed. The laugh brought a pain to his stomach and made him wince as he walked back to the sofa.

This was all too much for Momma. She stomped off toward Rell's bedroom, shouting his name again and again. Then she was pounding at the bedroom door.

"Your baby brother done got shot in his fuckin' stomach and you ain't got sense enough to watch over him? Open up this mothafuckin door, Rell. Right the fuck now, you hear me? Now!"

She kept pounding until Jah saw the light from inside Rell's bedroom spill out into the hallway as the door opened.

Jah grinned, suddenly entertained by his mother's rant. He found it hilarious. Countless times since childhood he could recall her cussing up a storm at Rell for not properly looking after him. It never got old.

She came back to the living room alone and scowling wonderfully.

"He gets that shit from Big Man," she said, holding her hips. "Lazy son of a bitch. Ain't got the sense God gave a dumb hoe. Stretch on out and lay down. You need anything?"

Jah didn't hesitate to lay out on the sofa and nod his head yes. "Some juice. I think it's some in the refrigerator."

"Rell!" Momma shouted at the top of her lungs. "Pour your brother some juice. Right. Fucking. Now. And tell that girl you got in there to come out here and meet the boss bitch around this muthafucka. Keep actin' like you don't know me, Rell. Keep on. I'll tear this muthafucka up."

Jah laughed again, longer this time, and put the gun on the table. This was getting too good.

Momma took off her coat and threw it on an easy chair. She was pissed off, and her expression showed it. She had on one of those hideous handmade holiday sweaters over faded jeans and Nikes. The same old gold watch Rell and Jah had gotten her for Mother's Day last year sparkled on her wrist.

"Rell, if I have to say it one more—" she started, but then Rell came walking out of his bedroom and into the kitchen.

Momma looked at Jah. "That nigga is so much like your dumb-ass daddy, I don't know what to do. Ugh."

Jah chuckled. "Calm down, Momma. I'm a'ight. I'll be good."

"You talk to ya daddy? Since you left the hospital, I mean."

"Nah. Rell talked to him."

"Boy, if you don't call that man and tell his ass you need some money. Hell, you can't afford to be moving around. Gotta pay somebody for the things you need. Don't be scared to ask that nigga for no money. He helped make you. That's his damn job."

This was nothing new to Jah. Money was always Momma's preferred topic of conversation. To her, everything was a reason to ask Big Man for some money.

He ignored her and watched the television. There were still no suspects in the murders. One eyewitness reported seeing several masked men appear from beside the house with guns blazing, but that was it. Jah was happy about that. Couldn't afford to have his big brother being sent away at a time like this.

Rell looked pissed off as he brought in a glass of orange juice and set it down next to the black box that held the submachine gun. He was only wearing a pair of gray mesh gym shorts and a pair of house shoes, and he smelled like good sex.

Momma rolled up her sleeves. "Sometimes I question if you're my son or not," she said, scowling at Rell. "I feel like I could go to the Maury Show tomorrow and he'd say, 'You are not the mother!' I really do."

Another laugh from Jah, and he wasn't the least bit surprised to see Rell laugh right along with him.

"Ma, you crazy as hell, you know that?" Rell sat down by Jah's feet. "I ain't gon' let nothin' happen to my lil brotha. I'm like All-state; he in good hands with me."

Maria scoffed. "Nigga, if you don't take that lame-ass quote back to the 1970s where you found it. What the hell you mean he's in good hands? I sure in the fuck can't tell. He's layin' there with a hole the size of Texas in his damn stomach."

Jah laughed until his stomach ached.

"Ma, will you please stop?" Rell handed Jah the glass of juice. "You gon' have him in even more pain."

Tamera came walking into the dining room, which was just off the living room, wearing jeans and a T-shirt, and Maria's attention shifted to her.

Rell's eyes got wide.

Jah's did, too.

So did Tamera's.

Momma balled up her fists, planted the knuckles of them on her hips, and glowered at Tamera.

"Have a seat at that table right there. Me and you need to have a talk."

Chapter 36

Reluctantly, Tamera sat down at the dining table, choosing the chair that was farthest away from Rell's mother. She regarded the older woman with a nervous smile, then lowered her eyes to her smartphone and finished typing the text she'd been getting ready to send to Tirzah.

"Sis where you at? It don't take that long to drive around the corner."

Instead of looking up at Maria — who was still going in on Rell about Jah getting shot — Tamera went to Facebook, for no reason other than to keep herself out of Maria's path.

Webb and Chino were all over her timeline. She went to Webb's Facebook page and saw heartfelt posts and condolences from his friends, family, and a number of girls he'd been messing around with before his death.

Among them was Sharon, the girl who Tirzah had beat the hell out of two days in a row. Sharon was Stain's daughter, and she'd also been one of Webb's side chicks. Her post read:

"Dam man this aint fare life aint fare man wtf!!! I luvd u w/ all of my hart web n u no it I luv u so much will miss u 4eva!! I'll alwayz b ur ladykakes!!!"

The post was followed by a hundred emojis. Sad faces, praying hands, hearts, broken hearts, kisses, heart eyes, crying faces, and more sad faces.

Tamera rolled her eyes and went to her own page. One of her old friends had tagged her in a funny video of a white girl threatening a black bear and then crying and begging him to stop when he attacked her canoe shortly thereafter. She would have laughed if not for the unwelcoming presence of Rell's mom.

There was another post on her page from Lenny, a guy she'd had a crush on since middle school.

"Hey, Tamsterr. Holla at the kid. I'm in from Vegas, won't be here but a week, would love to link up with you."

Just my luck, Tamera thought. Right when I find a man, the guy I've been wanting forever messages me for a date.

She liked the post and commented:

"Wish I could, friend. I really do. But I'm stuck in the house and at work this week. Maybe next time."

She was about to continue scrolling through other people's lives when suddenly the chair next to hers was pulled out.

She looked up just as Maria plopped down.

"Oh, Lord," she said, smiling nervously.

Maria did not return the smile. If anything, the smile made Maria's scowl deepen. She lit a cigarette and blew the smoke upward.

"Ma, don't be over there threatening my lady," Rell said from the living room.

Maria didn't even look Rell's way. Her cold brown eyes were unwaveringly glued to Tamera.

"So," Maria said, "tell me, what is it that made you wanna fuck my baby?"

The way Maria worded the question was funny. Tamera stifled a laugh.

"I'm not laughing," Maria said, not laughing at all.

"He's...I'm, uhh...I was single. He was single. You know how that goes, I'm sure. He seems like a good man, the kind of man I've been looking for. And in case you were wondering, I'm not a slut or a thot or none of those words. I hadn't had sex in a long time before him."

Tamera could not believe what she was saying. Admitting that she'd fucked this woman's son was more than she thought she'd have to say.

144

"It's okay, sweetheart. I'll tell you this much, and it's the truth, so help me God. Rell ain't no rolling stone, either. That damn girl Erica he was with wasn't worth the rubbers he fucked her with, because I can't count on all my fingers and toes the number of niggas she done slept around with, but Rell ain't never been like that. I can't speak for Jah, but that's just Jah. He'll fuck on anything with two legs. One day last summer he brought this great big ol' woman up in my house. Hoe smelt like green eggs and Spam, you hear me?"

Tamera busted out laughing, and this time Maria cackled, too.

"I'm so goddamn serious," Maria said. "But back to you. I only got two babies. Rell and Jah. They ain't much, but they're mine and I love 'em." She leaned over toward Tamera, voice low, the butt of her cigarette choking between her thumb and forefinger, as if she had somehow mistaken it for a blunt. "I'll tell you what God loves, and you can take this to the grave with you. Rell's a damn good man. I'm not just saying it because he's my baby. He used to be out in them streets like Jah is, and he'll get his hands dirty if it comes down to it, but I promise you, he's a good young man with an honest heart. He'll never lie to you, he'll always be there for you when you need him. He doesn't have a problem with making an honest living. One day he's gonna make some lucky woman a good husband, and if it's you, then I'm here to tell you that you've just met the man of your dreams. Treat him right and he'll treat you right."

"I will. No worries. Your son will be fine with me," Tamera said.

There was something in Maria's tone that told Tamera every word of what she'd just heard was the truth. The mother-to-step-daughter chat that she'd initially thought would be full of threats had turned out to be exactly what she wanted to hear.

According to Rell's mother, he was exactly the kind of man she was looking to spend the rest of her life with.

Maria got up and headed out the door, back upstairs to Jah's place.

Tamera walked to the living room and said, "Did Tirz say she was going somewhere else?"

145

"Nah," Jah said. "I was just thinkin' the same thing. I sent her a text. Just called her, too. She ain't answered, replied, or called back."

"That's not like her at all." A tidal wave of concern washed over Tamera as she dialed Tirzah's number yet again. "She always keeps that phone with her. I mean always. I can't think of the last time she's been awake and not had that phone in her hand."

When Tirzah didn't answer, Tamera panicked. Her heart started racing, her breathing quickened, and she ran to the living room window, praying that she would find Tirzah pulling up to the curb in Janky.

There was no red Taurus.

"Let me get dressed," Rell said. "As soon as Apple gets back with the food, we'll drive around there."

"Yeah," Tamera agreed. "Hurry up."

Two minutes later they were in their jackets and ready for the frigid winter air. Jah even threw on his jacket, saying that he'd join them.

Tamera stood at the window and waited for Rell's car to pull up. Only seconds had passed when she felt Rell's presence behind her. He put his arms around her waist, pressed his lips to the nape of her neck, and waited with her.

Chapter 37

Apple ended up getting everyone two Italian beef sandwiches apiece, including two more for himself. He went to King Gyro's on 16th, and when he got back in the car. he sat in the driver's seat and bit into one of his sandwiches.

"Bet a nigga won't get a bite of this one," he said, chewing. "Might take some bites out of theirs."

He was parked in the alley next to the restaurant, facing the street so that he could see everyone who drove and walked up.

He turned on the radio and rocked to an R. Kelly tune on 107.5 WGCI while he ate, looking around at the passing vehicles and pedestrians. He thought of his family and tried to decide if he should buy sandwiches for them, as well. The boys were fat guys like him, and they loved Italian beef sandwiches, especially with the special dipping sauce.

He would think on it more before he left. For now, he was focused on the sandwich at hand, which seemed to taste even better than the other two had.

He reclined the seat and got comfortable so that he could simply lower the sandwich to his mouth without being all up on the steering wheel. R. Kelly was singing about a body calling him. Apple thought that maybe he was being called by the sandwich.

He laughed at the idea and bit another chunk out of the fluffy wet bread and meat. He'd gotten green and red peppers, cheese, and tomatoes on the sandwich. It tasted like the perfect combination.

As he ate, his mind went to Rell and Jah and all the drama they were going through. He was glad that he wasn't involved in any of it. Not that he had never been in similar situations in the past. Apple had been in a few shootouts. He'd never killed anyone, but he knew that if it came down to it, he could. He'd chosen years ago to get away from that lifestyle, and he thought Rell had done the same thing. Actually, he knew Rell had done the same thing. It was Jah who was dragging Rell back into the streets, and by the looks of it, the new girl Rell had was the only thing keeping him in the house.

Apple stuffed a handful of fries in his mouth and chewed, shutting his eyes and thoroughly enjoying the scrumptious taste of them. He knew right then that he would be going back in for at least two more sandwiches before heading back to Rell's place.

He realized that the Kush had him feeling much higher than he usually felt after smoking on a loud pack. He tried to remember what kind of Kush it was. Jah had told him the name of it. Was it Jamaican Kush? Chinese Kush?

Another laugh burst out of Apple at the Chinese Kush idea. For all he knew, it could have been African Kush. He wouldn't be able to remember the name of the Kush until he either sobered up or asked Jah.

His smartphone was on the passenger seat, screen facing up so he would see if someone called. The notification light was blinking when he looked at it, which meant that he'd either gotten a text message or a Facebook Messenger message.

He was reaching over to grab the phone when someone knocked on his window. It didn't sound like knuckles on the glass. No, it was something solid, something that made a tink-tink-tink sound.

He turned to the driver's window and saw that it was Lil Chris.

Chris's battered and bruised face was nearly hidden inside a hoodie, and he had a gun in his hand — a big gun. Had to be a .45-caliber semiautomatic pistol.

Apple's heartbeat quickened, and his eyes grew wide as saucers. He'd known Lil Chris for years. The kid was dumb as a box of rocks but incredibly brave, as well.

"Ain't this Rell's car?" Chris asked.

Suddenly, Apple wished that he hadn't chosen to park in the dark alley. There were cars driving past on 16th, but no one was looking his way. Even if a cop so happened to drive by, he would be more focused on what was going on ahead of him and on the sidewalks. No one ever paid much attention to the alleys.

"You hear me, nigga?" Chris tapped the gun barrel on the window.

That was the tapping sound Apple had heard.

"Yeah. I, uhh...used his car...to come and grab a bite to eat."
He realized that he was stuttering but could not help it. "Listen, man,
I... I heard, um...I heard what happened. I'm not in that mess,
a'ight?"

Chris put the gun barrel on the window. "If you ain't in it, get
out the car and give me the keys. Tell me where Jah at."

Apple was full-on scared as he gathered up his phone and the
food and pushed open the door.

Chris stepped aside and kept the gun raised just high enough
to blow open Apple's stomach if he needed to.

"The keys is in the ignition, lil homie. You ain't gotta point
the gun at me. You know I ain't on that."

"I don't know what the fuck you on. You slidin' around in that
nigga's car. Say you know what's up. Playin' both sides."

"I ain't playin' no sides. I'm from out here just like you and
Jah is. Y'all got a problem. I'm not in it."

Chris didn't say another word. He got in the driver's seat of
the white Impala, aimed the gun at Apple, and opened fire.

Chapter 38

Susan's head was a lot clearer by the time she and Big Man walked into Top Burger.

The restaurant closed at midnight, and it was 11:45 P.M.

One female employee was mopping the red-and-white tiled floor. Whatever chemicals she'd put in the mop water had the place smelling good and fresh. She raised her head and gave a wave to Big Man and Susan as they passed her.

Susan ordered a bacon cheeseburger and Big Man went with the double. They sat down at a table and waited for their orders.

"You alright?" he asked, reaching across the table to hold her hands.

She nodded somberly. "I don't know what I was thinking, going to hang out with a drug addict. She stole everything I had."

"I see your jewelry's gone."

"I should find her and kill her." What Susan was really thinking was she should find that sneaky little rapist and kill him, but of course she could say no such thing.

"No, Suzie. Material things can be bought again. Just be glad that something worse didn't happen. Hell, getting drunk and going to sleep around people you don't know that well, it could have turned out a lot worse. You could've been raped, or even killed. Let's just thank God that you're okay."

Susan nodded her head, thinking, *I did get raped, jackass!* She was already thinking of what she would need to do about the rape. First thing tomorrow morning she would go and get herself checked out at the hospital. She'd say she and a friend had partied with some guys and neither of them remembered what happened. She'd get tested for sexually transmitted diseases and infections, and that was that. No more blind dates for her.

There was a football game playing on the wide-screen television beside their table. Big Man watched a few minutes of it while they ate. The employees stayed until halftime, which was at a quarter past midnight.

As they were leaving Top Burger, Big Man started rubbing at his chest. He stopped short of the car and bent over, one hand on a knee, the other on his chest. He belched.

"Heartburn. Jesus," he said.

She ripped the key to the car out of his hand and led him to the passenger door.

"No," he said. "You can't be drinking and driving." But both of them knew that his spells of heartburn could last a while.

She opened the door for him and he leaned on it, breathing, grimacing, panting.

"Just get in the damn car, Big Man."

He seemed hesitant but he folded under the steady pressure of her nudging him in the back and went ahead and sat down in the passenger seat.

Susan slammed the door shut and walked around to the driver's door, muttering, "This just ain't my damn day."

She got in and slid the seat forward. Big Man was so much taller than her.

"You're my blessing, Susan. For changing. For getting off the drugs," Big Man said. He reclined in the passenger seat and let out a second horrendous burp. "Jesus. That double cheeseburger did a number on me."

"You're my blessing, too." Susan leaned toward him and gave him a kiss on the cheek. "Fat man."

"I pray that my boy's okay."

Susan pulled back quickly. Luckily it was dark, or else Big Man might have seen the hatred on her face.

The boys this, the boys that — everything was always about those fucking boys. She'd just gotten drugged up and raped, for Christ's sake, and the only thing on this asshole's mind was his boys.

"They're both grown men, David. Grown. You know what that means? It means you let them go and focus on your wife." She started the engine, grinding her teeth together.

"I'm just worried about Jah," Big Man said. "He's been shot. Ain't no way I can sit here and not think about that. That's my baby boy, you know? I didn't get a daughter. Gotta cherish what God gave me."

"Yeah, well, God also gave you a wife who needs cherishing."

"And I do cherish you, Susan. I really do. The thing is, you weren't shot today. My son was. Show some consideration. Everything can't be about you."

Susan's teeth were still grinding together as she drove out of the dimly lit parking lot and onto 1st Avenue. She was tempted to sock Big Man square in the mouth for what he'd just said. She was feeling terrible about the hotel incident. Sure, there was no way she could tell him the truth, but he wasn't being caring enough about the whole robbery story, either.

Now she didn't feel so bad about the date with "Chuck", even though it hadn't turned out as she'd hoped it would.

She sighed and shook her head. *Maybe some music will help,* she thought.

She looked to the radio and saw four knobs where before there had been two. She gasped and looked up.

There were three identical trucks coming right at her.

"David!" she shouted, just half a second before the crash.

Chapter 39

"I sent Apple three texts, and I just called twice. The nigga ain't answered yet." Rell turned to look at Jah, who was lying on the sofa with his eyes on the ceiling.

"What y'all wanna do?" Jah asked.

"I'll walk," Tamera said.

Rell shook his head. "I'll go up and get Momma's keys. We can take her truck."

He went upstairs to Jah's new apartment and found Maria fast asleep on the sofa. He took her keys off the table and left back out as quickly as he'd come.

Maria's whip was an off-white Mercury Mountaineer. She kept it spotless both inside and out. Jah took to the backseat and held the Mac-10 on his lap, and Tamera sat up front next to Rell as he turned the key in the ignition and waited for the SUV to warm up.

In the rearview mirror, Rell saw two police cars race past on 16th Street.

Tamera phoned her sister again and then dropped the phone in frustration when she got no answer.

"Something is definitely wrong," she said. "She always answers that damn phone. Fuck."

Rell drove off down Trumbull, going much faster than he usually drove. No one spoke as he turned onto 15th and then onto Homan and finally onto 16th.

The first thing they noticed on 16th Street was a swarm of police cars that were crowded in front of the King Gyro's restaurant five blocks to the left of them. Rell immediately feared the worst for Apple, and he wanted to make a left turn to go and see what had happened, but he made the right turn that would lead him to Shalonda's house on St. Louis Avenue.

Rell rolled down his window and slowed down as he was passing Meeko, an older guy he'd known for years. Meeko seemed to be in a hurry. He was jogging toward St. Louis.

"Ay, Meeko. What happened back there? Where all those police at?" Rell asked.

"You know Apple, don't you? Fat boy off Trumbull? Somebody clapped the homie up, joe. Did him bad. They don't think he gon' live."

Rell's heart sank. He flicked his eyes over to Tamera and then back to Meeko. "Was he in a car?"

Meeko shook his head no. "Nope. He was laid out in the alley, joe. They just put him in the ambulance. It's all bad. I'm on my way down to Central Park to let his sister know now."

"Oh, my God," Tamera murmured.

"Damn," Jah said from behind Rell.

Tamera convinced Rell that it was a good idea to report his car stolen before any crimes could be committed in it. He was hesitant to deal with the police, but she was right. He had to report the Impala stolen, especially if he wanted to benefit from his car insurance. He made the call as they were pulling up onto 16th and St. Louis.

There was no red Ford Taurus parked in front of Shalonda's house. The house lights were off.

"Bruh, if Shalonda done set some bogus shit up, she gettin' it off top," Jah said as Rell parked.

Tamera jumped right out and ran up onto the porch. Rell and Jah were seconds behind her, Rell with his Glock in hand, Jah clutching the Mac in his jacket.

She banged on the door.

Rell looked around, wondering what the fuck was going on. Someone had shot Apple. It had to be because of the car Apple had been driving. No one in the streets had any kind of beef with Apple. He was the fat, funny friend who kept everybody laughing. He'd rarely even gotten into fights.

No one answered Shalonda's door.

Tamera's expression became a fiery mask of rage. She stepped back, getting ready to kick the door.

Then her phone rang.

Rell looked at the screen as she took the smartphone off her waist.

156

He saw Tirzah's contact picture.

Chapter 40

"Bitch, I know you saw me calling!"

Zo cracked a smile. He had it on speakerphone. He was sitting in the passenger seat of PJ's chameleon-painted Tahoe, which was parked behind his new Chevy in the pitch-black alley on 13th and Avers.

They were right behind Jah's mother's house, where PJ's uncle had been killed.

Tirzah was in the trunk of the Chevy, probably still unconscious from the beating PJ had given her.

PJ looked over at him and silently mouthed, "Is that Tamera?"

Zo nodded his head.

Taking a hit of the blunt he'd just rolled, he said into the phone, "Bitch, watch yo' mu'fuckin' mouth. You don't even know who the fuck you talkin' to."

He heard her gasp.

"Who is this? Where's my sister?"

"That's the million dollar question right there, ain't it?" Zo smiled at PJ as he passed the blunt. "I'll tell you this much: wherever the bitch at she ain't happy."

"Who...who is this?"

"It's your worst nightmare, hoe. Where them hoe-ass niggas you been hangin' wit'? You tell me where to find 'em and I'll tell you where to find yo' sister."

The next voice Zo heard belonged to none other than Jahlil Owens.

"What up, nigga? You lookin' for me?"

Zo was almost too afraid to reply. His eyes got wide. He looked over to PJ again, but this time there was no amusement in his eyes; only fear. Pure, unfiltered fear.

For years, Zo and his close friends had regarded Jah with the highest level of fear imaginable. They'd heard stories of how Jah had gunned down men in broad daylight when he was only eleven and twelve years old. Everybody who knew Jah feared him, so much so that most people refused to even speak his name.

Zo didn't know what to say. "I, uh...where you at?" Zo said.

PJ frowned and snatched the phone from Zo's hand. "Lil nigga, come over here to your momma's house. I got some holla for you."

"I'm on my way!" Jah ended the call abruptly.

PJ stared at Zo as he handed the phone back. "The fuck you freeze up for?"

"I ain't freeze up, nigga."

"Well, what you call that shit you just did? Scary-ass lil nigga."

Zo shook his head. "You don't know Jah like I know Jah. That nigga's a hitta, joe. On Neal. He gon' come through this bitch sprayin' on sight. I'm telling you what I know."

"Nah. Not while we got his girl. You just be ready with that Tec. Empty the whole clip at that nigga soon's he pull up. Get out and duck off next to that garage right there. Hurry up."

Zo didn't argue with PJ, mostly because he didn't want to be anywhere in sight when Jah showed up.

"You heard what I said," PJ reminded Zo as he hopped out of the passenger seat. "Don't do no hesitatin'. Just blast on that nigga. Kill him and whoever with him, then we'll off that bitch and get the fuck up outta here. I got some big money put up. I'll look out for you. Plus, I'll take you to Georgia with me and show you some real money once this shit is over. First thing's first, though. We murk this nigga, then we hit the highway and ball out."

Zo gave an unsure nod and pushed the door shut. As he walked to the side of Jah's mother's garage and ducked low beside the bushes, heart pounding like a drum in his chest, eyes flicking every which way, fingers wrapped tightly around the Tec-9 submachine gun he'd gotten from Webb, he thought back to when Chris had first come up with the idea to rob Jah's brother. He wished that he would've talked Chris out of it. They would've been better off just robbing Webb.

He took out his smartphone and dialed Chris's number, quickly shutting off the screen once the ringing began to keep anyone from seeing the glow of it in the darkness.

Chris answered. "Bruh, I clapped that nigga Apple up. Caught him in Jah's brother's car. Made him get out, then I baked him with my brother's fo' nickel." Four nickel was street slang for a .45-caliber handgun.

"You wet Apple up? Fat Apple, off Trumbull?"

"Yeah. Ain't that what I just said? He was in that Impala. I baked his cake and took that mu'fucka. Ridin' around with E right now."

"Man, y'all dumb as hell. Get the fuck out that hot-ass car, nigga. Meet me on 13th and Avers right now. I mean right the fuck now. It's about to go down any second. We got Jah on the way over here. We gon' light his ass up, then we can get low to Atlanta."

"Atlanta? We don't know nobody in Atlanta, nigga, is you nuts?"

"It's a long story, bruh. But put it like this. We on. We got racks. Told you I came up earlier, bought a Chevy and everything, on Neal."

Chris laughed. "You's a mu'fuckin' lie, but a'ight. I'm on North Avenue. About to head that way now. You said Avers?"

"Yeah. On 13th. Just look for the white Chevy and the chameleon Tahoe in the alley. And hurry up, bruh. I'm serious. Speed, nigga."

Zo put the phone in his pocket and lit a cigarette. It was cold out. The news he'd seen at Shalonda's house had said 24 degrees.

Knowing that he was squatting in the bushes behind the very same house he'd shot up earlier made him uneasy. He worried that police could possibly be somewhere in the distance, watching the house to see what was going on.

His mind went to Tangie. She had stayed in the house with Shalonda. He wondered if him picking her up in the Chevy would be an everyday thing.

The memory of how she'd looked as she got in the car with him brought a grin to Zo. Seeing him dressed clean and riding clean had put a glorious smile on the popular girl's face. For the first time since he'd laid eyes on her, she actually looked at him with interest.

Suddenly, Zo felt compelled to contact Jah and apologize for his role in the robbery attempt. That way he'd be able to spend all the money he'd gotten from Webb in peace. PJ had beef with Jah over a murder; none of Zo's friends had been murdered.

The Tec-9 became ice-cold in his hands. The frigid air numbed his lips around the cigarette. He squatted there thinking for a while, considering if he should find a way out of this mess or do as PJ had said and just light up whatever car Jah arrived in.

Chapter 41

"It's a setup. That was PJ on the phone. I met him at a party once. That's his voice. He's Sharon's cousin, Stain's nephew." Tamera spoke in a low, thoughtful tone, keeping her eyes on the road as she raced toward 13th Street in Maria's SUV. She had tears running down her face but she was focused.

Rell and Jah were in the back seats behind her, their guns on their laps, eyes on their windows.

"The first voice was Zo," Jah said.

"If they've done something horrible to my sister, I'm killing them myself," Tamera said.

Rell reached around the driver's seat and squeezed her shoulder. "We got this, baby. Slow down before you get there. Don't pull up in the alley. That's what they want us to do. Park two blocks down and we'll walk the rest of the way. You just stay in the car and wait for us to get back. We'll find Tirzah."

Tamera shook her head. "No. Hell no. I'm going. That's my big sister."

Rell sighed but he didn't repeat his suggestion. He understood Tamera's determination. Tirzah was her sister and she wasn't about to just sit by while some guys she'd only recently met tried to save her sister's life.

He turned back to his window just as Tamera made it to Independence Boulevard, and what he saw made his mouth fall open.

His Impala was veering around his mother's SUV, right alongside his door.

"These niggas right here! Look at this shit!" he said, pointing at his car in disbelief. "Just follow them."

"They've gotta be the dumbest criminals in the world," Tamera said as she got on their trail. "These have got to be the guys who shot Apple."

Jah nudged Rell with an elbow and picked up the Mac-10. "What up, bruh? Wanna shoot that mu'fucka up or what?"

"That's your car, bruh," Rell said. "Pops said I can get the Escalade when they get back from Florida as long as I give you the Impala."

Jah put down the Mac, and Rell shook his head. The little fucker was all the way with shooting up the Impala until he found out it was his.

Tamera fell back a few car-lengths from the Impala and stayed on its trail. It proved to be quite the obstacle. The Impala was moving forward recklessly, sliding across patches of ice and sleet as it went.

Once they were two blocks away from Maria's house, Rell told her to pull over and park, and they watched the Impala as it went straight to the corner of 13th and Avers and made a turn.

"They're going to the alley—" Rell said, and then he froze as the booming sounds of gunfire filled the air.

Tamera shut off the headlights and drove off toward the gunshots.

Chapter 42

The recoil from PJ's .45 threw off his aim as he stepped out of the Tahoe firing round after round at the Impala, not even giving its driver time to park. He wanted Jah and Rell dead, and he was going to get it done himself this time. No more fuck ups.

He glanced at the bushes next to the garage just as Zo emerged from them wielding the Tec, and then quickly shifted his attention back to the Impala as it went crashing into a garage door further down the alley.

PJ was enraged. His upper teeth sank down into his bottom lip as he filled the car with bullet holes. He saw whoever was in the passenger seat slump over and stop moving. He hoped that it was Jah.

"Hoe-ass niggas!" he shouted - just seconds before he felt the sting of bullets tunneling through his own body.

Out of the corner of his eye, right before he collapsed to the snow-covered ground, he saw the flash of Zo's Tec-9 firing and immediately knew that it was trained on him.

Chapter 43

Zo panicked when he saw that PJ was shooting at the Impala. E and Chris were in the Impala!

He turned the Tec on PJ and squeezed the trigger until the clip was empty. By then PJ was on the ground, frantically kicking his legs and rubbing his large hands over the holes in his chest and stomach.

Zo ran up on PJ and picked up the .45, simultaneously dropping his own gun in the process. Then he ran to the Impala, choking back tears as he noticed that E was slumped over with his brains blown out in the passenger seat, and that Chris had pushed open the driver's door, but was also slumped over and hanging halfway out of it.

Zo was on the verge of breaking down in tears as he walked around the front of the car and squatted down at the driver's door beside Lil Chris, who was gasping for breaths, his eyes rolled up in their sockets.

There was a nickel-sized hole in the side of Chris's neck, and several more in his coat.

"It's my fault, bruh. Damn," Zo said, lifting Chris's head in his arms. "I didn't tell him y'all was on the fuckin' way! Shit!"

Chris died in Zo's arms, and Zo kept holding him, rocking back and forth and shaking his head, muttering "Shit" again and again until the word was no more than a hoarse whisper.

He finally found the strength to stand up. His knees had hardly straightened when he felt the barrel of a gun against his temple, and he heard the one voice he was most afraid of say, "You know you done fucked up, don't you?"

Chapter 44

"No, Jah! We have to find my sister! Zo, where's my sister?!" Tamera shouted.

Rell heard Tamera pleading with Jah to spare Zo's life for the moment but he was far too busy making sure the others were no longer threats to pay any attention to her.

He was standing over a dead fat guy — PJ? — when he heard a thumping sound coming from the trunk of the white Chevy Caprice. Just then, he heard Zo tell Jah that Tirzah was in the trunk.

Rell went to the driver's door, opened it, and popped the trunk. By the time he made it back around to the rear of the Caprice, Tirzah was climbing out of the trunk, with Tamera holding her forearm until her sneakers were planted on the ground. Tirzah's jaw was swollen, her nose was bleeding, and there was a knot over her left eye.

Police sirens were closing in fast.

Jah had Zo lying face-down in the snow. "Y'all come on so I can whack this lil nigga," he said.

"Nah, bruh," Rell said as he and the girls rushed to his mother's SUV. "You don't hear those sirens? Twelve on the way. Let's go, nigga. Catch that lil nigga later."

In the streets of Chicago, "twelve" was code for police.

Rell could tell that it ate Jah up to leave Zo alive, but he listened and walked backward to the rear driver's side door of their mom's SUV, which he'd left open.

Tirzah got in next to Jah, and Tamera veered off in reverse, whipped around on the street, and then put it in drive and headed back in the direction from which they'd come.

Rell chuckled as he realized what had happened in the alley before they pulled up. PJ had seen his Impala and shot it up without a second thought, not knowing that the boys in it weren't Jah and Rell. When Zo had seen PJ shooting up the Impala, he'd shot PJ dead.

"Dumb-ass niggas killed each other before we could even get to 'em," he said, looking back at Jah and Tirzah.

Tirzah had her head in Jah's lap. She was crying, holding her jaw, wiping away the tears. Jah planted a kiss on the side of her head and rubbed her shoulder. It was a sweet scene, despite the circumstances. Rell wasn't used to seeing his younger brother showing emotion. Usually Jah didn't spend more than a single night with a girl before he kicked her to the curb.

Tamera was also crying. Rell's eyes moved to her tear-streaked face, then to the diamond ring on her finger. She was up close to the steering wheel, her fingers curled tightly around it.

A police car sped past with its lights flashing brightly. Seconds later another one lanced by, then two more.

Tirzah said, "It was that bitch Shalonda. She had to have set it up. They came right at me."

Tamera only nodded and gripped the steering wheel in an even tighter embrace. She was obviously upset, and if Jah could console Tirzah, then he was supposed to be consoling his girl, too.

At the next red light, he grabbed her by the chin, turned her face to his, and kissed her. It was a long, calming, heartwarming kiss that lasted until the light turned green.

Tamera gazed at Rell as he pulled back.

"We got this, baby. Just drive."

The Nissan behind them honked, and Tamera regained focus. She drove off through the intersection.

"Thanks," she said. "I needed that. I really did."

They were back on 16th Street when Rell said, "Where you going?"

Tamera laughed once. "Where do you think we're going? To that bitch Shalonda's house. She knew what the fuck was going down. She set up my sister, and now she's going to pay for it."

Chapter 45

Shalonda had all of the lights turned off. Her kids were with her mother, which was a good thing, because she didn't know how this night would play out. Especially with Jah in the mix.

She and Tangie were in her bedroom, illuminated by just the light of her television and the screens of their smartphones. They were sipping on some Ciroc vodka, smoking the bullshit weed that Tangie had gotten from one of her friends, and scrolling through Instagram.

"That was so fucked up," Shalonda said. "The way PJ was beating on that girl when they dragged her out the car. I felt so bad for her. That's somebody's daughter."

Tangie sucked her teeth. "Girl, boo. Fuck Tirzah and her bum-ass sister. They think they the shit 'cause they got ass and hips. Broke-ass bitches ain't no different from nobody else out here."

"She still didn't deserve to get treated that way. I don't care how stuck up she is. She's a woman. I'ma have a long talk with PJ about that shit soon's he get here."

Tangie gave another suck of the teeth and went back to studying Instagram. They were both on The Shade Room's page, enjoying all the latest industry gossip and viral videos. There was an adorable new video clip of Chris Brown and his daughter that the two of them just could not stop watching. Another video from a while back, showing a Black kid threatening to beat up a group of white kids, sent them rolling over with laughter.

Then came a rough knock on front door.

Shalonda gasped and quickly shut off the TV to extinguish the small amount of light there was in the room, just as she'd done when someone banged at the door about twenty minutes earlier. She knew that her mom would call before stopping by, and that PJ had a key, so she didn't care who the visitor was. She wasn't going to answer it. Not when she'd practically just set up Jah's girlfriend.

The knocks progressed to vicious bangs that brought another gasp from Shalonda, then the banging stopped just as suddenly as it had begun.

"Somebody knows what happened with Tirzah," Tangie said. "I'd bet money on it. Nobody's ever banged on your door like that, and this is the second time it's happened in less than an hour. Nobody bangs on doors at two o'clock in the morning unless it's serious."

"Shut up, Tangie."

"You know I'm right. You shouldn't have done that."

"What did I do? Huh? I didn't do a damn thing, so shut up."

"You tried to call Jah over here."

"Yeah, Jah. Not Tirzah."

"But you knew she was coming. And when they snatched her out of that car, you drove it down the street to hide it."

"No, what I did was drive it down the street to get it out from in front of my damn house. That's what I did. Shit, I hope you don't tell the police all that. Nosy ass lil girl. Find you some fucking business."

Shalonda didn't want to admit that she was scared out of her mind. Her sister was right. She should never have gotten involved in the plot against Jah. She'd watched a dozen episodes of The First 48 where the girl was hit with the same charges as the men for setting someone up. If PJ and Zo had taken Tirzah somewhere and killed her, then Shalonda was just as guilty for luring Tirzah to the house as they were for killing her.

Shalonda's phone rang a few seconds later. It was Saidah, a Muslim girl she'd worked with at Pizza Hut last year. Saidah lived over on 13th Street. Shalonda didn't know exactly where, since she'd never bothered to pay Saidah a visit. Sometimes she and PJ saw Saidah whenever they stopped by Pizza Hut, but that was about it.

Saidah sounded frantic. "Hello? Shalonda?"

"Yeah, it's me. What's going on?"

"I don't know how to tell you this but...PJ is, um...he's laying in my alley. Cops are everywhere. I was in bed asleep when the shooting started."

"Wait, what do you mean laying in your alley? Is he alright?"

"I don't think so, Shalonda. Looks like he's...you know. Dead."

Shalonda paused for a long moment, not sure if she should cry her eyes out or pack her bags and get out of town. She decided to do the packing now and the crying later. She thanked Saidah for the information, ended the call, and immediately went to her closet, stopping to turn the TV on for the light.

She dragged out PJ's heavy suitcase first, knowing that it was where he kept his cash stashed away. Then she took another suitcase and began filling it with clothes.

Meanwhile, Tangela just sat on the bed and sipped from her cup of vodka, as if she had no idea what was going on.

"Get dressed, Tangie," Shalonda said.

Tangela looked at Shalonda like she was crazy. "Dressed? Bitch, it is two o'clock in the morning, not to mention the fact that you've got some unknown psycho knocking at your door. No, I'm not getting dressed to go anywhere. You go by yourself if you wanna go somewhere. I'll wake up in the morning and take my—"

"PJ's dead, Tangie." Shalonda put her hands on the hips of her pajama pants and stared at Tangela. "Somebody killed him in the alley on 13th. Now, I know for a fact that there's at least a hundred thousand dollars in this suitcase of his. We can take this shit and go, or I can take this shit and go. It's up to you."

Tangie looked at the suitcase. "A hundred grand?"

"Ain't that what I just said?"

"In that suitcase?"

"Bitch, if you ask me another dumb-ass question I'm leaving without you. Get dressed. We can leave and get ourselves a hotel room, then we can just leave first thing tomorrow. I'll pay Ma a few grand to keep the kids until we get back. Come on and get dressed, now. We ain't got all damn day. Ain't no telling if the cops gon' come running up in here."

Tangie stood up beside the bed, still eyeing the suitcase. "I wanna see it," she said. "I wanna see the money first. If you show me the money, I'll go."

"Fine. Help me lift it up onto the bed. And you got five seconds to look and another five seconds to get ready to go."

They hefted the heavy brown leather suitcase onto the bed, and Shalonda unzipped it.

This would be her first time actually seeing it open herself. Usually PJ only went in it when he was alone in the bedroom. He'd said that it was none of her business how much money he had in it, that as long as he took care of the bills she should mind her business.

She was shocked to find so much cash inside the suitcase.

"Oh, my God," Tangie said.

There were bundles of hundreds, fifties, and twenties, all held together with rubber bands and stacked on top of each other. Shalonda picked up one of the cash bundles and fanned through it in disbelief. Tangie did the same thing.

"This is a lot of fucking money," Tangie said. "Holy shit, sis. Fuck me. This is real fucking money."

"Yeah, it is. Told you." Shalonda snatched the cash from Tangie's hand, tossed it back in the suitcase, and zipped it shut. "Let's hurry up and get out of here before whoever that was banging at my door comes back."

She and Tangie dressed hurriedly, and just ten minutes later they were leaving out the back door, on their way to better days.

Chapter 46

Better days were not to come. Not for Shalonda and Tangela. After finding her car abandoned a block down from Shalonda's house with the keys still in the ignition, Tamera had driven it into the alleyway behind Shalonda's house and waited patiently, while Rell and the others waited out front in Maria's SUV. Out of frustration, she had gotten out of the car, walked around to the front door, and pounded on it like a madwoman before returning to Janky and again waiting.

She had just pushed open her door again, this time with the intent to break into the house like she'd wanted to do from the start, when she saw the rear porch light turn on and two girls come rushing down the stairs with two suitcases.

Tamera had never shot a gun in her entire life, but the 9 millimeter pistol she'd taken from Webb was in her left hand, and she could think of no better time to start shooting it than now.

Shalonda and the girl who was helping her with one of the suitcases didn't notice Tamera's presence until they were just ten feet away from her.

She had the gun aimed right at them.

"I didn't have nothing to do with it, Tamera!" the girl with Shalonda said, and hearing the voice made Tamera realize that it was Tangela, a young girl she knew from seeing around the neighborhood. She'd heard that Tangela was Shalonda's sister, but had never known for certain if it was true or not.

"Bitch," Tamera said to Shalonda, slowly walking forward, her sneakers crunching in the snow, "you set my sister up? Do you have any idea how much I love my sister? They beat my sister and put her in the trunk of a car. Bitch!"

Shalonda could only hang her mouth open in shock.

"Listen," Tangela said, letting go of the suitcase and holding her hands out pleadingly. "She's got a ton of money in—"

"Shut up." Shalonda gave Tangela an elbow to the ribcage. "Look, Tamera, I'm sorry, okay? I didn't know what was going down. He told me to call Jah for some weed, and that's what I did. Your beef ain't with me..."

Tamera wasn't listening to a word of Shalonda's explanation. She was more focused on what Tangela had just said about the ton of money.

"Open those suitcases before I shoot both of you bitches," Tamera said, squinting. She wanted to phone Rell and tell him to come back here and join her but she didn't want to risk it. For all she knew, one or both of the girls could be strapped.

Suddenly, Shalonda's expression shifted from one of fear to one of anger. She regarded Tamera with a heated scowl.

"Look, Tamera. I'm not afraid of you. Your sister shouldn't have been dropping off drugs for a nigga like Jah in the first place. Everybody knows he's a dead man walking, and you hoes are dumb for even talking to him. He's gonna end up dead just like Stain."

"And PJ. Let's not forget him," Tamera retorted. "He's dead, too, you know."

Shalonda let go of the suitcases and bolted toward Tamera, arms outstretched as if she planned to grab ahold of Tamera's neck when she got close enough.

Tangela shouted, "No, Londa!"

BOOM! BOOM! BOOM!

Three loud explosions of gunfire cracked open the silence of the night. Each round found its mark in Shalonda's chest.

Tangela screamed and leapt on top of her sister, sobbing uncontrollably. "The money's in the suitcase!" she shouted hysterically. "Just take it and leave!"

"Which suitcase?" Tamera's voice was remarkably calm.

"The brown one! Now go! Please!" Tangela yelled.

Tamera nodded her head twice, took a few seconds to think things through, and then shot Tangela in the side of the head. She then stood over Shalonda and gave her a headshot, as well.

"Dumb-ass bitches. Nobody hurts my sister and gets away with it," Tamera said, dragging the brown leather suitcase to her car.

She managed to get the suitcase onto the backseat without needing help, but it left her a little out of breath.

She dialed Rell's number and told him to drive around to the alley and follow her home, ignoring his questions when he inquired about the gunshots.

King Rio

Chapter 47

Rell didn't ask Tamera about the big brown suitcase when she had him carry it to his bedroom and set it down at the foot of the bed; it was a quarter to three in the morning, and both of them were dead tired.

They put their smartphones on the charger on the nightstand, stripped down to their undies, and got under the covers. Tamera threw a leg over his legs and an arm over his chest and put her jaw on his shoulder.

"I offed those bitches," Tamera said.

Rell felt tears sliding down into his armpit. He rubbed Tamera's shoulder and gave her a kiss on the forehead.

"Fuck 'em, baby. They deserved it."

"She rushed at me. I wouldn't have done it if the bitch would've just followed orders. I wasn't there to do that. I'm not that type of person."

"Don't let it get to you, baby."

Tamera sighed. "It's all over now, ain't it? I mean, PJ's dead, Webb's dead. Those boys who tried to rob you looked pretty damn dead to me."

"Zo. He's still out there. Might have to give his lil ass the blues, but yeah, guess it is over. Jah and Tirzah might take a little while to heal all the way up but they'll be good. We're alive, and we're together. That's what counts most, ain't it?"

"Yeah." She sighed. "I suppose it is."

"It is. Just...let's just get some rest. We'll talk about it in the morning."

"Wait."

"Wait? For what?" Rell asked.

"Before we go to sleep. Before we dream."

"What?" he repeated.

"I know that we haven't known each other all that long, but as you can see from all the shit we've already gone through I'm a down-ass chick. I'm someone worth loving."

"I agree. I think every black woman is worth loving."

"Well, can you do me a favor? Just for tonight?"

"What kinda favor?"

"Can you tell me you love me? Even if you don't mean it. I just really need to hear it. I've never heard it before bed, and if there was ever a time I needed to hear it it's now." She cocked her head back to look at him, and he gave her lips the firmest of kisses.

"I love you, you beautiful woman. Loved you ever since I first saw you open that door at your apartment the other day. It was love at first sight."

Tamera made a soft whining noise and pecked her lips against his again before moving the side of her face back to his shoulder.

Jah and Tirzah were in bed together in Jah's bedroom upstairs.

Tamera nodded her head a couple of times and snuggled up closer to Rell. She slid her left hand across his chest, back and forth, back and forth, and the last thing Rell remembered seeing before sleep took him was the 9-carat white diamond ring on her finger.

Chapter 48

When Rell's eyes fluttered open five hours later, he thought he was still dreaming.

The bedroom door was shut. The television was on and tuned to CNN (Anderson Cooper and Kathy Griffin preparing for the countdown to their 2016 New Year's Eve special). And there was cash all over the floor on his side of the bed.

Tamera was on her knees tending to the stacks of cash, counting through a bundle of hundreds. She had on a white shirt over white leggings, and her hair was wrapped in a white Gucci scarf.

Rell sat up, confused.

Tamera looked up at him and smiled.

"Good morning to us!" she chirped, throwing a triumphant fist in the air. "$188,475 so far! Shit, Tirzah wasn't lying! That fat nigga was holding out! And look over there." She pointed to two big blocks of cellophane-wrapped dope on the dresser. "I'm not sure, but I think that's a lot of heroin sitting up there. Jesus, this guy was loaded!"

Rell got out of bed in a hurry and snatched up a pile of hundred-dollar bills. He flipped through the cash in utter disbelief.

"This shit gotta be counterfeit or somethin'," he said, already wide awake, even though he had not had his usual eight hours of sleep. "All this was in that suitcase? Damn, no wonder it was so heavy."

"I know, right!" Tamera was full of cheer. "And I'm not even done counting it all yet! Looks like at least twenty or thirty thousand more. I'll let you know the exact amount. Go and get yourself together. Brush your teeth, too. Yuckmouth."

Rell laughed and went to the nightstand to get his smartphone and his .40-caliber Glock pistol. He didn't want to leave the room, fearing that the money would somehow disappear if he let it out of his sight.

He had four missed calls from a number with a 305 area code. He hurried into the bathroom and brushed his teeth, then took the quickest shower of his life and returned to the bedroom with a bath towel wrapped around his waist.

The money was still there. Tamera was still counting it. She looked up at him again, this time shaking her head and smiling her beautiful smile.

"What did you think I was gonna do, jump out the damn window with the money?" she asked.

He chuckled and sat down on his side of the bed to put on a pair of boxers. "Nah, I just can't believe it. I ain't never seen that much bread in my life. Did you show it to Tirzah and Jah?"

"Nope. They haven't even come down here yet. Your mom did, before she left for work. Said she'd go and get her work uniform herself since you forgot to do it."

"Fuck that uniform. We can buy her a new uniform."

"We?"

Rell furrowed his brows. "Yeah. Hope you don't think it's all yours."

A sweet giggle blew from Tamera's lips. "Just joking, fool. We can all split it — me, you, Tirz, and Jah. We deserve it after all the shit we've been through this week. I'm definitely getting rid of Janky and getting me something clean."

"I don't know about splitting it, either," Rell joked as he swiped on some deodorant and set his phone back on the nightstand. *I'll return the missed calls in a few minutes*, he thought.

Tamera tossed aside the rest of the cash and stood up. Her curvaceous body, and the fact that there were obviously no underwear under the leggings, made Rell's chest expand with a deep breath. She sat on his lap and pressed her lips to his.

"Good morning, my king," she said. "I lost count at $190,000. We'll each get around $50,000. I don't want anything to do with that dope, though. I don't want you dealing it, I don't want Jah dealing it. If you want it, have somebody else do the selling."

"Sounds like good advice." Rell kissed the side of her neck and slipped his fingers down into the rear of her leggings. He shut his eyes and inhaled through his nose. He wasn't sure if Tamera was wearing perfume or not but whatever it was had her smelling good enough to eat.

He turned and threw her to the bed, stepping back to shut the door.

"I was waiting on this," she said, and quickly peeled off the leggings. "Just got out the tub, too. It's nice and fresh for you. Get to eating, dear."

Rell dropped his head back in laughter. "You know you got me fucked up, right?"

"I ain't got you fucked up. Nigga, you saw Booty Call, didn't you? 'You got to lick it, before you stick it!' You better stick to the code!"

Biting down on his bottom lip, Rell moved on top of her and pushed up her shirt. He sucked and licked on one nipple for a few seconds, then did the same to the other, then went down for an unofficial breakfast between her thighs.

He loved the taste of her. He could think of no better taste than Tamera's juicy nookie. He gripped her thighs in his hands and buried his face in her pussy, sucking her clitoris and digging his tongue inside her, inhaling the scent that was more delicious than any meal.

As she dug her fingernails in the back of his head, it occurred to him that he needed a haircut. He would go and get one today, with Tamera by his side, then he'd be by her side as she got her hair and nails done, then they'd go shopping and splurge a little.

Yes. Today would be a great day.

He pushed her legs up and tongued her to an orgasm that made her scream and push away from him and fall onto the piles of cash next to the bed.

"Why you runnin'?" He chuckled, looking down at her and grinning widely. "Get back up here, nigga."

Tamera shook her head and held up an index finger. "Wait. When I catch my breath, and when my legs stop shaking, your ass is grass."

"And let me guess: you're the lawnmower, huh?"

She nodded, sitting up and breathing hard, looking so beautiful that Rell had to pause and stare. A strip of sunlight spilled through the curtain and put a magical glow on her skin. The sunshine also reflected off the diamond ring, making it sparkle brilliantly.

His dick was fully erect and trying its best to bust out of his black boxers. He pulled it out and stroked it.

A couple of seconds passed before Tamera finally got up and climbed back onto the bed.

"Let me get that backshot action, baby," Rell said, because he loved the view of her from the back.

Tamera wasn't one of those girls who didn't know how to look sexy in the doggystyle position. She kept her face down and her ass up, her back arched perfectly. She looked over her shoulder at him as he fucked her. It was the sexiest position ever, in Rell's opinion.

She seemed to know exactly what he was thinking, because she got in front of him, put her head down on her pillow, and lifted up her generous derrière.

Rell smacked the crown of his pole-hard phallus on her cotton-soft buttocks before sliding inside of her.

Her pussy was virgin-tight, sopping wet, and so warm that Rell had to wait a few seconds before he started thrusting just to keep himself from ejaculating prematurely.

His smartphone rang just as he started sliding in and out of her, and he didn't even look to see who was calling. He rubbed the palm of one hand across Tamera's lower back and fucked her roughly, loving the sound of her fluctuating moans.

They were facing the side of the bed where the cash was stacked up. Rell gazed fixedly at the money. Close to a quarter of a million dollars. He could not believe it.

He smiled, feeling much better than he'd felt yesterday. He had about $50,000 cash to himself, and the reality of it was almost too good to be true. The thought that maybe he was still dreaming crossed his mind, but he knew that he was indeed awake. This was very much real.

About ten minutes passed and then Tamera wanted to get on top to ride him. He lay on his back and stared up at her as she mounted him. He cupped her breasts in his hands as she impaled herself on his dick and started bouncing. She dropped all her weight down and winded her hips, gasping and breathing heavily. It was obvious that the sex was just as good to her as it was to him.

She planted her feet on either side of him and started slamming down, moaning so loudly that Rell thought the neighbors might file a complaint. He held her hips in a firm grip and shut his eyes.

"Yes, yes, yes!" Tamera yelled, clawing at his chest and moaning incessantly.

She rode him for a long while.

His smartphone rang again on the nightstand, and again he ignored it.

He rolled over, putting Tamera on her back and shoving her legs so far up that her toes touched the headboard.

Her screaming moans grew louder. Rell slammed deep inside her with every thrust until his scrotum lifted and twitched. He bit her bottom lip between his teeth and kept sliding in and out of her as his semen escaped and filled her womb. She dug her fingernails in his back, and her mouth stayed open.

When he finally rolled over on his back, panting and feeling relieved, the two of them gazed into each other's eyes until their breathing stabilized.

"You are the best, Rell. I really mean that. Fuck. My legs are shaking so bad right now," Tamera said.

"I'll take that as a compliment." Rell chuckled. He was sweaty and ready to go back to sleep. "You okay? About last night, I mean."

"Yeah." She nodded, and raised her left hand to look at the ring. "I'm good. What happened is what happened, you know what I mean. Can't change the past. All we can do is try to make today a better day than yesterday."

"You really like that ring, don't you?"

"Like? More like love! You see I haven't taken it off since you let me try it on."

"I gotta mail that off to Suzie today. She's been bugging the fuck outta my pops for it."

Tamera sighed. "I know. It's so beautiful. I wish it was mine." She turned back to him. "If we ever get married, you're getting me a ring like this one."

"Is that a suggestion or a demand? Damn."

"Both." Tamera snickered joyfully and kissed his shoulder, then hopped up and left the bedroom. "I'm about to cook breakfast. Feel free to get a few more Z's in. I'll wake you up when the food's ready."

Smiling, Rell reached over to the nightstand and grabbed his phone, wondering what city had a 305 area code. All he knew was 773 and 708.

He returned the call and was surprised to hear a white man answer.

"Hello? Somebody called me from this number?" Rell said.

"Yes, may I ask who I'm speaking with?"

"This Rell."

"Oh. Well, Rell, I'm Detective Johnson of the Miami Police Department. Are you related to a David or Susan Owens?"

"Yeah." Rell sat up, frowning. "David's my pops. Why, what's going on?"

"Found your number in your dad's phone. Your father and his wife were in a car accident at around midnight last night. Collided head on with a semi. I'm sorry to tell you this, but...neither of them survived the crash."

To Be Continued...
Mobbed Up 3
Coming Soon

Submission Guideline

Submit the first three chapters of your completed manuscript to ldpsubmissions@gmail.com, subject line: Your book's title. The manuscript must be in a .doc file and sent as an attachment. Document should be in Times New Roman, double spaced and in size 12 font. Also, provide your synopsis and full contact information. If sending multiple submissions, they must each be in a separate email.

Have a story but no way to send it electronically? You can still submit to LDP/Ca$h Presents. Send in the first three chapters, written or typed, of your completed manuscript to:

LDP: Submissions Dept
Po Box 944
Stockbridge, Ga 30281

DO NOT send original manuscript. Must be a duplicate.

Provide your synopsis and a cover letter containing your full contact information.

Thanks for considering LDP and Ca$h Presents.

Coming Soon from Lock Down Publications/Ca$h Presents

BLOOD OF A BOSS **VI**

SHADOWS OF THE GAME II

TRAP BASTARD II

By **Askari**

LOYAL TO THE GAME **IV**

By **T.J. & Jelissa**

IF TRUE SAVAGE **VIII**

MIDNIGHT CARTEL IV

DOPE BOY MAGIC IV

CITY OF KINGZ III

By **Chris Green**

BLAST FOR ME **III**

A SAVAGE DOPEBOY III

CUTTHROAT MAFIA III

DUFFLE BAG CARTEL VII

HEARTLESS GOON VI

By **Ghost**

A HUSTLER'S DECEIT III

KILL ZONE II

BAE BELONGS TO ME III

A DOPE BOY'S QUEEN III

By **Aryanna**

COKE KINGS V

KING OF THE TRAP III

By **T.J. Edwards**

GORILLAZ IN THE BAY V

3X KRAZY III

De'Kari

KINGPIN KILLAZ IV

STREET KINGS III

PAID IN BLOOD III

CARTEL KILLAZ IV

DOPE GODS III

Hood Rich

SINS OF A HUSTLA II

ASAD

RICH $AVAGE II

By Troublesome

YAYO V

Bred In The Game 2

S. Allen

CREAM III

By Yolanda Moore

SON OF A DOPE FIEND III

HEAVEN GOT A GHETTO II

By Renta

LOYALTY AIN'T PROMISED III

By Keith Williams

I'M NOTHING WITHOUT HIS LOVE II

SINS OF A THUG II

TO THE THUG I LOVED BEFORE II

By Monet Dragun

QUIET MONEY IV

EXTENDED CLIP III

THUG LIFE IV

By **Trai'Quan**

THE STREETS MADE ME III

By **Larry D. Wright**

IF YOU CROSS ME ONCE II

By **Anthony Fields**
THE STREETS WILL NEVER CLOSE II
By K'ajji
HARD AND RUTHLESS III
Von Diesel
KILLA KOUNTY II
By Khufu
MOBBED UP III
By King Rio

Available Now

RESTRAINING ORDER **I & II**
By **CA$H & Coffee**
LOVE KNOWS NO BOUNDARIES **I II & III**
By **Coffee**
RAISED AS A GOON I, II, III & IV
BRED BY THE SLUMS I, II, III
BLAST FOR ME I & II
ROTTEN TO THE CORE I II III
A BRONX TALE I, II, III
DUFFLE BAG CARTEL I II III IV V VI
HEARTLESS GOON I II III IV V
A SAVAGE DOPEBOY I II
DRUG LORDS I II III
CUTTHROAT MAFIA I II

KING OF THE TRENCHES

By **Ghost**

LAY IT DOWN **I & II**

LAST OF A DYING BREED I II

BLOOD STAINS OF A SHOTTA I & II III

By **Jamaica**

LOYAL TO THE GAME I II III

LIFE OF SIN I, II III

By **TJ & Jelissa**

BLOODY COMMAS I & II

SKI MASK CARTEL I II & III

KING OF NEW YORK I II,III IV V

RISE TO POWER I II III

COKE KINGS I II III IV

BORN HEARTLESS I II III IV

KING OF THE TRAP I II

By **T.J. Edwards**

IF LOVING HIM IS WRONG…I & II

LOVE ME EVEN WHEN IT HURTS I II III

By **Jelissa**

WHEN THE STREETS CLAP BACK I & II III

THE HEART OF A SAVAGE I II III

By **Jibril Williams**

A DISTINGUISHED THUG STOLE MY HEART I II & III

LOVE SHOULDN'T HURT I II III IV

RENEGADE BOYS I II III IV

PAID IN KARMA I II III

SAVAGE STORMS I II

AN UNFORESEEN LOVE

By **Meesha**

A GANGSTER'S CODE I &, II III

A GANGSTER'S SYN I II III

THE SAVAGE LIFE I II III

CHAINED TO THE STREETS I II III

BLOOD ON THE MONEY I II III

By J-Blunt

PUSH IT TO THE LIMIT

By **Bre' Hayes**

BLOOD OF A BOSS **I, II, III, IV, V**

SHADOWS OF THE GAME

TRAP BASTARD

By **Askari**

THE STREETS BLEED MURDER **I, II & III**

THE HEART OF A GANGSTA I II& III

By **Jerry Jackson**

CUM FOR ME I II III IV V VI VII

An **LDP Erotica Collaboration**

BRIDE OF A HUSTLA **I II & II**

THE FETTI GIRLS **I, II& III**

CORRUPTED BY A GANGSTA I, II III, IV

BLINDED BY HIS LOVE

THE PRICE YOU PAY FOR LOVE I, II ,III

DOPE GIRL MAGIC I II III

By **Destiny Skai**

WHEN A GOOD GIRL GOES BAD

By **Adrienne**

THE COST OF LOYALTY I II III

By Kweli

A GANGSTER'S REVENGE **I II III & IV**

THE BOSS MAN'S DAUGHTERS I II III IV V

A SAVAGE LOVE **I & II**

BAE BELONGS TO ME I II

A HUSTLER'S DECEIT I, II, III

WHAT BAD BITCHES DO I, II, III

SOUL OF A MONSTER I II III

KILL ZONE

A DOPE BOY'S QUEEN I II

By **Aryanna**

A KINGPIN'S AMBITON

A KINGPIN'S AMBITION **II**

I MURDER FOR THE DOUGH

By **Ambitious**

TRUE SAVAGE I II III IV V VI VII

DOPE BOY MAGIC I, II, III

MIDNIGHT CARTEL I II III

CITY OF KINGZ I II

By **Chris Green**

A DOPEBOY'S PRAYER

By **Eddie "Wolf" Lee**

THE KING CARTEL **I, II & III**

By **Frank Gresham**

THESE NIGGAS AIN'T LOYAL **I, II & III**

By **Nikki Tee**

GANGSTA SHYT **I II &III**

By **CATO**

THE ULTIMATE BETRAYAL

By **Phoenix**

BOSS'N UP **I , II & III**

By **Royal Nicole**

I LOVE YOU TO DEATH

By **Destiny J**
I RIDE FOR MY HITTA
I STILL RIDE FOR MY HITTA
By **Misty Holt**
LOVE & CHASIN' PAPER
By **Qay Crockett**
TO DIE IN VAIN
SINS OF A HUSTLA
By **ASAD**
BROOKLYN HUSTLAZ
By **Boogsy Morina**
BROOKLYN ON LOCK I & II
By **Sonovia**
GANGSTA CITY
By **Teddy Duke**
A DRUG KING AND HIS DIAMOND I & II III
A DOPEMAN'S RICHES
HER MAN, MINE'S TOO I, II
CASH MONEY HO'S
THE WIFEY I USED TO BE I II
By Nicole Goosby
TRAPHOUSE KING **I II & III**
KINGPIN KILLAZ I II III
STREET KINGS I II
PAID IN BLOOD **I II**
CARTEL KILLAZ I II III
DOPE GODS I II
By **Hood Rich**
LIPSTICK KILLAH **I, II, III**
CRIME OF PASSION I II & III

194

FRIEND OR FOE I II
By **Mimi**
STEADY MOBBN' **I, II, III**
THE STREETS STAINED MY SOUL I II
By **Marcellus Allen**
WHO SHOT YA **I, II, III**
SON OF A DOPE FIEND I II
HEAVEN GOT A GHETTO
Renta
GORILLAZ IN THE BAY **I II III IV**
TEARS OF A GANGSTA I II
3X KRAZY I II
DE'KARI
TRIGGADALE I II III
Elijah R. Freeman
GOD BLESS THE TRAPPERS I, II, III
THESE SCANDALOUS STREETS I, II, III
FEAR MY GANGSTA I, II, III IV, V
THESE STREETS DON'T LOVE NOBODY I, II
BURY ME A G I, II, III, IV, V
A GANGSTA'S EMPIRE I, II, III, IV
THE DOPEMAN'S BODYGAURD I II
THE REALEST KILLAZ I II III
THE LAST OF THE OGS I II III
Tranay Adams
THE STREETS ARE CALLING
Duquie Wilson
MARRIED TO A BOSS I II III
By Destiny Skai & Chris Green
KINGZ OF THE GAME I II III IV V

Playa Ray
SLAUGHTER GANG I II III
RUTHLESS HEART I II III
By Willie Slaughter
FUK SHYT
By Blakk Diamond
DON'T F#CK WITH MY HEART I II
By Linnea
ADDICTED TO THE DRAMA I II III
IN THE ARM OF HIS BOSS II
By Jamila
YAYO I II III IV
A SHOOTER'S AMBITION I II
BRED IN THE GAME
By S. Allen
TRAP GOD I II III
RICH $AVAGE
By Troublesome
FOREVER GANGSTA
GLOCKS ON SATIN SHEETS I II
By Adrian Dulan
TOE TAGZ I II III
LEVELS TO THIS SHYT I II
By Ah'Million
KINGPIN DREAMS I II III
By Paper Boi Rari
CONFESSIONS OF A GANGSTA I II III
By Nicholas Lock
I'M NOTHING WITHOUT HIS LOVE
SINS OF A THUG

TO THE THUG I LOVED BEFORE

By Monet Dragun

CAUGHT UP IN THE LIFE I II III

By Robert Baptiste

NEW TO THE GAME I II III

MONEY, MURDER & MEMORIES I II III

By **Malik D. Rice**

LIFE OF A SAVAGE I II III

A GANGSTA'S QUR'AN I II III

MURDA SEASON I II III

GANGLAND CARTEL I II III

CHI'RAQ GANGSTAS I II III

KILLERS ON ELM STREET I II III

JACK BOYZ N DA BRONX I II III

A DOPEBOY'S DREAM

By **Romell Tukes**

LOYALTY AIN'T PROMISED I II

By Keith Williams

QUIET MONEY I II III

THUG LIFE I II III

EXTENDED CLIP I II

By **Trai'Quan**

THE STREETS MADE ME I II

By **Larry D. Wright**

THE ULTIMATE SACRIFICE I, II, III, IV, V, VI

KHADIFI

IF YOU CROSS ME ONCE

ANGEL I II

IN THE BLINK OF AN EYE

By **Anthony Fields**

THE LIFE OF A HOOD STAR

By **Ca$h & Rashia Wilson**

THE STREETS WILL NEVER CLOSE

By **K'ajji**

CREAM I II

By **Yolanda Moore**

NIGHTMARES OF A HUSTLA I II III

By **King Dream**

CONCRETE KILLA I II

By **Kingpen**

HARD AND RUTHLESS I II

MOB TOWN 251

By **Von Diesel**

GHOST MOB

Stilloan Robinson

MOB TIES I II

By **SayNoMore**

BODYMORE MURDERLAND I II III

By **Delmont Player**

FOR THE LOVE OF A BOSS

By **C. D. Blue**

MOBBED UP I II

By **King Rio**

KILLA KOUNTY

By **Khufu**

BOOKS BY LDP'S CEO, CA$H

TRUST IN NO MAN

TRUST IN NO MAN 2

TRUST IN NO MAN 3

BONDED BY BLOOD

SHORTY GOT A THUG

THUGS CRY

THUGS CRY 2

THUGS CRY 3

TRUST NO BITCH

TRUST NO BITCH 2

TRUST NO BITCH 3

TIL MY CASKET DROPS

RESTRAINING ORDER

RESTRAINING ORDER 2

IN LOVE WITH A CONVICT

LIFE OF A HOOD STAR